# B.U.G.
# (Big Ugly Guy)

# B.U.G.

## (BIG UGLY GUY)

### Jane Yolen
AND
### Adam Stemple

DUTTON CHILDREN'S BOOKS

*An imprint of Penguin Group (USA) Inc.*

DUTTON CHILDREN'S BOOKS
*A division of Penguin Young Readers Group*

Published by the Penguin Group
Penguin Group (USA) Inc., 375 Hudson Street, New York, New York 10014, U.S.A.
Penguin Group (Canada), 90 Eglinton Avenue East, Suite 700, Toronto, Ontario, Canada
M4P 2Y3 (a division of Pearson Penguin Canada Inc.) | Penguin Books Ltd, 80 Strand,
London WC2R 0RL, England | Penguin Ireland, 25 St Stephen's Green, Dublin 2, Ireland
(a division of Penguin Books Ltd) | Penguin Group (Australia), 707 Collins Street,
Melbourne, Victoria 3008, Australia (a division of Pearson Australia Group Pty Ltd) |
Penguin Books India Pvt Ltd, 11 Community Centre, Panchsheel Park, New Delhi - 110
017, India | Penguin Group (NZ), 67 Apollo Drive, Rosedale, Auckland 0632, New Zealand
(a division of Pearson New Zealand Ltd) | Penguin Books (South Africa), Rosebank
Office Park, 181 Jan Smuts Avenue, Parktown North 2193, South Africa | Penguin China,
B7 Jiaming Center, 27 East Third Ring Road North, Chaoyang District, Beijing 100020,
China | Penguin Books Ltd, Registered Offices: 80 Strand, London WC2R 0RL, England

CIP Data is available.

Published in the United States by Dutton Children's Books,
a division of Penguin Young Readers Group
345 Hudson Street, New York, New York 10014
www.penguin.com/youngreaders

Designed by Irene Vandervoort

Printed in USA | First Edition

ISBN 978-0-525-42238-9

Special Markets: 978-0-735-23225-9

10 9 8 7 6 5 4 3

*There are rivers in the world, with their banks*
*a particular type of clay. Form this clay into the*
*semblance of a man, and place a piece of paper with*
*God's ineffable name written upon it in Hebrew under*
*the creature's tongue, and you shall bring forth a*
*golem. And he shall not eat, nor drink, nor accept any*
*pay, but he will protect you from harm and do your*
*work and your bidding.*

*Until he doesn't . . .*

# B.U.G.
## (Big Ugly Guy)

## Before

*2008: In an underground research facility,*
*near Rehovot, Israel*

Chaim crouched in the men's room in the dark and prayed. He wasn't particularly religious—he was a scientist, after all, in his first year of real work.

But this night was different from other nights. It was Passover. And it was definitely a night for prayer.

He shuddered as the sound of automatic gunfire rattled down the long hallways, accented by the booming reports of a single .50 caliber Desert Eagle.

*Guns won't stop the protectors*, he thought. *The soldiers don't know what they're fighting.*

Chaim knew, though.

"It's *keshaphim*," he whispered into the dark. "Magic."

But it had all started with science.

Chaim had always been good at science. Had a gift

for it. Since grade school, he could see patterns in raw data that other people needed weeks to decipher. He had the ability to explain his results clearly to any audience.

When you have such a gift, Chaim felt, you should use it in service. Give back to those who had educated you. So when the secret service, known as the Mossad, came to him before he even started fielding offers from the private sector, he listened.

"There's money in the big companies," they told him, "but there is no *kavod*, no honor."

Remembering the recruiters' words now brought a cheerless smile to his face. *Where's the honor in waiting in the dark to die?*

Back then, it had seemed not just an honor but a joy to come to work every day. He was in the technology department. The equipment was cutting edge, the staff dedicated, and his bosses wanted him to think and act "outside of the box." No idea was too wild to mention, and most of the time he was encouraged to follow up on even the craziest of them. So when he began seeing patterns in historical data pointing to something outlandish, unbelievable, even . . . mythical . . . he was still allowed to perform some experiments.

His boss, a man named Lev Spiegel, laughed as he signed the paperwork.

"Should I call you Rabbi Loew?" he said.

Rabbi Loew. The sixteenth-century chief rabbi of Prague. The one who created a creature from clay to defend the Jews in the ghetto. A creature called a golem.

"Let's see if it works first," Chaim replied.

Lev was the first in Chaim's department to die. Then Nissa, his research assistant. Then . . .

*Then the rest of them*, Chaim thought as the gunfire stopped. *There's nobody left but me.*

And now heavy footsteps were heading for his hiding spot. But instead of fear, Chaim suddenly felt strangely calm.

*Kavod*, he thought. *If I am to die, I won't die in the bathroom. I will do it with honor.*

He stood. Opened the stall door. Felt his way in the dark toward the exit. Toward the footsteps. When he stepped into the corridor, he could see again. Small fires were crackling where gunfire had set stacks of paper or garbage alit, illuminating the area.

*Thwop . . . thwap . . . thwop . . . thwap.* Slow stone footsteps on cement floors.

They were coming.

Chaim shuddered but moved with a purpose to the nearest pile of papers strewn on the ground. Gathering them up, he fed them into one of the fires, then bent and grabbed more. He added those as well, and within moments, the flames were tall enough to lick the ceiling. As he turned to build another fire, he saw long shadows starting to creep around the corner. He scurried wildly around now, tossing papers onto every flame he could see.

"I will burn this place to the ground!" he shouted at the shadows. "No one will know what happened here."

He expected no response from the shadows or the creatures casting them. And he didn't get one. Just the slow, relentless approach of their footsteps.

*Thwop . . . thwap.*

"No one will repeat this deed!"

*Thwop . . . thwap.*

They were around the corner now and in full view, but Chaim didn't look up. He knew what they looked like. What they were.

"And if I survive," he said softly, "I will leave this desert and move somewhere cold and wet." He fed a last piece of paper to the flames. "And I will study the Torah every day."

Then he looked up into the lifeless eyes of the creatures he'd created and started toward them.

He was thinking of the name of God.

*Another Day in the Boys' Room*

Sammy Greenburg was head down in the boys' toilet. Again.

He knelt on the cold gray tiles until the laughter faded and the footsteps left his side. Until the boys' room door snicked shut. Until he stopped shaking with anger and fear.

He'd just sat back on his bottom, wringing his wet curly hair on the bowl's edge, when the door opened.

*Not more,* he thought. *One swim a day in the porcelain pool is enough. And this time it wasn't just because he'd mouthed off at James Lee and his cohorts.* Cohorts. *He loved that word. Sounded like something full of ugliness and warts. And not because of a paper he'd been forced to write for James Lee which got James Lee a D plus. On purpose. After all, Sammy knew the teacher would figure out right away that James Lee hadn't read the book* Frankenstein. *All the references were to movies like* Young Frankenstein *and to actors like Boris Karloff. He was proud of that. It took a kind of warped genius to pull off.*

"*My* warped genius," he whispered.

*No, this time he'd been dunked because he'd stood up for Bobby Marstall, a seventh grader whose lunch money was about to get pocketed. Did* get *pocketed. So he'd achieved nothing but a dunking and it was the worst one yet. He really thought he was going to be drowned this time.*

"I *am* nothing," he said softly to himself in a frothy way, spitting out toilet-bowl water as he spoke. As he waited for yet another dunking.

"Are you, like, okay?" The voice was soft, concerned.

Sammy glanced up and snapped, "Do I look, *like*, okay?"

"You look, like, damp." It was the new kid, his dark face and chocolate-brown eyes full of concern.

"I *am* damp." Sammy squeezed more water out of his hair. "This isn't perspiration." *Perspiration* was one of his favorite words. Other kids said sweat. But not Sammy.

"Come on," the new kid said, "let's wash your hair in the sink. God knows what's been in that bowl."

"God knows, and now I know, too," said Sammy. "And it wasn't anything good." *Better the sink*, he thought, not knowing whether the new boy was going to be *like* the rest of them.

Bending over, Sammy rinsed his hair out and then washed his face and ears. The new kid helped, directing the water flow by sticking his finger up into the faucet. It was freezing cold—but no colder than the water in the toilet. *And a lot cleaner!*

"Here," the kid said, when Sammy was done. He handed him a strange-looking narrow black metal comb with widely spaced teeth. "All I have."

"Thanks." Sammy tried to get his hair to part properly with the comb, failed, then handed the comb back. He thought a minute. Considered alternatives. Finally he said what was really on his mind. "Okay, level—why are you helping me? Trying to soften me up for another swim?"

"Oh, was that swimming?" the kid said. "It looked more like drowning." He put his head to one side as if considering, then added, "Actually I was just coming into the bathroom for, like, other reasons. But recon in a new school is always helpful."

"Recon?" Sammy wasn't sure he knew what that

meant, which was strange. He was always the kid with the largest vocabulary in any school he'd ever attended. One of the other reasons he'd been head down again in the toilet. James Lee Joliette had called him a backstabber when the *Frankenstein* paper had come back, and when Sammy had replied, "Better than a backwoods yahoo." He hadn't expected to get away with it. Even if it was true.

This time he'd gone even further, trying to divert attention from little Bobby Marstall. Called James Lee "a backstreet bank robber with a degree in thuggery and a brain the size of a macadamia nut," which even made some of his gang start to snicker. It had given Bobby time to run off after giving up his lunch money. *Which,* he thought, *probably makes me some sort of a hero. Or some kind of idiot. Or a healthy helping of both.*

"Recon," Sammy said again, trying to parse the word. He hated not knowing the meaning.

"Reconnaissance." The kid shrugged—almost an apology. "Dad was in the army. Like a major. He's out now. And none too soon, Mom says."

Sammy wiped his face with the sleeve of his left hand. *What a terrific word,* he thought: *Reconnaissance.* He'd only seen it written, never spoken aloud. Except in war movies. And he didn't get to go to many of them. Or see them on TV either since they hadn't had a TV the past three years. His mother's decision, but neither he nor his father ever watched much TV anyway. They were all readers. He held out his right hand. "Sammy Greenburg. Thanks."

"Funny last name."

Sammy stiffened. That's what the other boys always said. In a town full of Joliettes, Arnettes, and Von Pattens, his name invited jokes about what part of him was green. His only edge in this place was his wit and his fast tongue. "You think Greenburg's a funny name?"

"No—but *Thanks* is."

Sammy laughed. This guy was tongue-fast, too. Maybe he wouldn't be as bad as the rest.

The new kid held out his hand. "Call me Skink."

"Isn't that a lizard?" Sammy was all ready to follow that with something snappy about lizards, though he wasn't actually sure what kind of lizard a skink was, when the new kid interrupted his thoughts.

"*Real* name is Skinner John Williams after my grandfathers. But everyone just calls me Skink."

Admiringly, Sammy shook Skink's hand. "Okay, Skink. I'm named after my great-grandfather, too. Samson." He made a face. "I'd rather you didn't tell anyone."

"Like, would someone named Skinner make fun of a name?"

"Guess not. You'd just get landed with Skin-and-Bones and Skinny Minny and . . ."

"And Skinflint."

"Really? Not around here. No one would know what that means."

"You do," Skink said. It wasn't a question.

"Yeah," Sammy said. "A skinflint is a miser, someone who squeezes a nickel to get back change." Back at his last school there was someone who had called him that. Even though Sammy really didn't have any money to speak of. He'd just assumed it was an anti-Semitic remark. Not one of the worst, of course. He could live with it.

"Well, Word Man, meet the Skink," the new boy said.

Sammy grinned. *Word Man.* He liked that. Could own it!

Just then the bell rang for the start of classes.

"I'm in Holsten's homeroom," Sammy said, starting

to hurry down the hall. Skink was moving in the same direction, but Sammy's brief hope of actually having a friend in his homeroom was quickly crushed.

"Not me. I've got Lippincott."

Sammy made a face. "Sorry. He's tough. Big, too."

Shrugging, Skink said, "It, like, doesn't matter. Small school. I'm sure we'll have some classes together. If not, I'll see you at lunch!" Then he waved and turned down the hall toward Mr. Lippincott's room.

Waving back, Sammy ran to his first class.

Ms. Holsten was slim and blond and not bovine in the least. Not that this stopped her from being known as "Holstein," to most of her students. With a name like Holsten in dairy cow country, what do you expect? But she remained pleasant and soft spoken and tolerant of all kinds of behavior, especially the stuff that could be expected from a classroom of unruly eighth graders. Like fart jokes and armpit noises, gossiping, occasional fits of the giggles, and an awful nickname.

Except for tardiness. Sammy knew she was never tolerant about tardiness. And Sammy was tardy. *A dip in the ceramic swimming pool can do that to you*, he thought. Not very tardy, mind you. Just a touch after the bell. A smidgen. A mere iota. But that little bit was enough for Ms. Holsten.

"Mr. Greenburg." His name suddenly had a lot more syllables than Sammy remembered. Ms. Holsten drawled it out until the whole class was staring. "Are you late?"

"Only a little, Ms. Holsten. I had to . . . erm . . . wash my hair."

There were sniggers from some boys in the back of the room. Giggles from the girls. Sammy wasn't sure which was worse.

Word gets around quickly. These weren't even the boys who'd dunked him. Dunked him because he'd gotten in their way. Because he stood up for someone who couldn't stand up for himself.

*Nah*, Sammy thought, having one of those revelations that comes after a near-death experience. *They dunked me because I'm different. Because I'm not one of them. And because . . . they can.*

In fact, it had taken James Lee less than a week to decide that Sammy was different. Sammy's name was one indicator. And he didn't go to church, either. Not James Lee's Baptist church, or the smaller Catholic church at the end of town.

"You must be one of them furrin immigrants," James Lee had said to Sammy the first week of school.

Not realizing that James Lee was someone you didn't want to butt heads with, someone who had absolutely no grasp of irony, had never spoken anything with the sarcasm font, Sammy had replied, "Yeah, I immigrated all the way from Hartford."

"Where's that at?"

"Connecticut." And then Sammy added—which was another big mistake, since he was not only dissing James Lee, but where he lived—"It's one of the earliest states in the USA, in case they don't teach that here. One of the original colonies. More American than the Midwest. Those thirteen stars on the first American flag? Connecticut was one. I was born there. And my parents. Both of them. And my grandparents. We're not the foreigners." He pronounced it properly and with particular care and compounded the mistake by pointing at James Lee. "You are."

He didn't add that since his birth, they'd moved six times, each time farther and farther away from Hartford so his potter father could find a big enough and cheap enough place to build his pottery. Though his dad sold pots to major stores all across America, room for an outsize studio and a stand-alone wood-fire kiln was hard to find in their budget which, as far as Sammy could tell, was one step above the poverty line. One small step.

That time, James Lee had pushed Sammy down, stepped over him, and at the same time had laughed. "Furriner. Can't fool me. Catch that name? Greenburg. BURG! Leave out the r and what do you have?"

When his friends looked blank, he added, "BUG, that's what. He's a green bug. And you know what we do to them?"

If anything, the blank stares got blanker.

"We squash 'em!" And James Lee had laughed.

Only then did his friends laugh with him. "BUG!" they shouted. And from then on, that was what they called Sammy. They'd been shouting it when they'd sent him swimming in the porcelain pool.

"Sammy!" Ms. Holsten snapped, and Sammy realized he'd missed whatever she'd said next.

"Oh, sorry, Ms. Holsten. What did you say?"

"I said, since it's you, no detention." There were mutters from the back of the room. Sammy could just make out the words "teacher's pet."

This day just keeps getting better.

He sighed. "Thank you, Ms. Holsten."

She gave him a thin smile. "Don't let it happen again."

At least, he thought, there would have been some dignity in detention. The cool kids seemed to get detention as a matter of course; they did whatever they wanted and their school day was just a half hour longer. Sammy could have sat in detention and hung out with them. Explained that he had nothing against them, and shown that he got in trouble, too.

But he knew instinctively things would never happen that way. He just couldn't resist talking back to the bullies. Cutting them down with his tongue. If he could only learn to suffer in silence, they'd probably get bored and turn on someone else.

*Being quiet's just not in my DNA*, he thought, all the while doubting that any of the boys who had dunked him had a clue as to what DNA was.

Besides, he told himself, by missing detention I can get home before they get out. Because most of them are in detention every day. And that's in *their* DNA.

Then he had a darker thought. Better watch out at lunch.

Lunch was a jostling, shoving scrum, where kidney punches could be delivered with no teacher the wiser.

Besides, the food could be spit on, sneezed on, boogered, soiled. And there was the long, lonely walk while carrying a tray full of food back to his seat, dodging legs that suddenly shot out to trip him.

Yes—lunch could turn out to be even worse than the trip home on the bus. At least there, the driver—a hairy man named Baer who looked like he really did have bears somewhere on his family tree—kept order by turning his head and growling at any misbehavers. Sammy had actually considered bringing him a jar of honey but had resisted the idea at the last moment. He wasn't sure Mr. Baer's sense of humor was any more advanced than the Boyz.

A few hours later, when Sammy entered the cafeteria, he realized that today's lunch was going to be different.

Very different.

Because his tormentors had found a new target.

Skink.

By Sammy's estimation, Skink had made three rather
large mistakes.

*Number one*, he'd sat down at the center table.
Everyone knew that table was reserved for James Lee
Joliette and his ninth-grade crew. Even if Skink hadn't
known anything about them, he should have recognized
their *clubbiness* by their leather jackets and combat boots
and by their hair, cut as short as their tempers. *Clubbiness*
might not be a real word, but Sammy thought it fit. They
were the Toilet Dunkers Club.

*Number two*, Skink hadn't moved when Joliette and crew
showed up. He might have been let alone if he'd admitted
his mistake, being a new kid and all. If he'd laughed at

their jokes about him, stood up and found another seat, preferably one on the other side of the room, close to the door. But Skink seemed to be content to sit and pick at his meal while James Lee loomed over him, yelling in his ear.

*He doesn't even have the sense to look scared,* Sammy thought.

*Third mistake*—and, Sammy figured, probably the most important—Skink had been born black. A light black. Sort of a hot chocolate with lots of cream color. He had strange lozenge-shaped eyes. Sammy didn't believe in aliens, and sometimes wasn't entirely sure about God, either. However there was something wonderfully, comfortingly alien about Skink in the sea of pasty white faces in the lunchroom.

But James Lee hated people who were different. James Lee's father was well known in town for his drunken tirades about what "furriners" had done to this country, meaning anyone who hadn't lived there, in Hicksville, for at least three generations. James Lee had obviously inherited his old man's views.

Sammy's dad had smiled when he first heard this and said, "We're in the middle of the Midwest. What immigrants is he worried about? Canadians?"

Sammy's mother had laid a hand on his shoulder. "Us," she said.

With Skink, the differences were all right out there on display. James Lee didn't need a week to discover them.

"You're at my table, kid," James Lee said. "You're in my seat."

However, Skink didn't look offended or upset or scared, all of which made sense to Sammy. *He looks kind of . . . peaceful.* Sammy gulped. *He must not realize the danger he's in.*

"Okay, listen—if you don't get up on your own, I'm gonna have to make you." James Lee's voice cut like a knife across the lunchroom. Everyone heard it.

The prospect of James Lee making Skink move seemed to cheer his crew and a few of them began to grin.

"Up!" one of them added, and giggled. It was a surprisingly high giggle, and he was rewarded with an elbow in the side by one of his pals.

"Shut up, Marv," the elbower said.

Now, Sammy knew that James Lee was a lot of things. Most of them bad. But Sammy had no reason to

think of him as a liar. If he said he was going to make
Skink move, then Skink was going to get moved.

*It's simply a law of nature, like gravity,* Sammy thought.
*Or tornadoes.* They knew a lot about tornadoes in that
part of the Midwest.

If James Lee didn't move Skink himself, his crew
would. Individually, they were already the size of most of
the seniors and already all on the football team, not just
James Lee. Next year, James Lee, like his older brothers,
was sure to be a starter. After all, his uncle Billy Jack
Joliette was the secondary coach.

"You've got till the count of three."

Skink moved his tray to one side.

"One . . ."

*I've got to help him!* Sammy thought. *He's got to get out
of there!*

"Two . . ."

*Here goes nothing. . . .* Sammy opened his mouth to
shout, though he wasn't quite sure what would come out.
He was certain that after the shout—which was just to
get everyone's attention, like the old joke about hitting
a mule on the head with a two-by-four—there would
have to be some begging and then something amusing.

Something *very* amusing. Often Sammy could get out of the worst of things by making James Lee and his cronies laugh. *As long as the joke is on somebody else.* They had absolutely no sense of humor about themselves.

Whatever he did, though, Sammy knew he had to do it soon. After all, Skink was someone who might become a friend, and Sammy didn't want to see him hospitalized on his very first day.

Sammy cleared his throat. It wasn't quite a shout, but nonetheless it worked. For a second, James Lee turned toward him.

"James Lee," Sammy began, "Skink . . ."

"Shut up, Bug," James Lee suggested.

Before Sammy could get anything else out, Skink looked over and shook his head.

"I got it, Sammy," he said. And stood up.

James Lee smiled like a snake—all thin lips and no teeth. "Good choice. I'd hate to mess you up on your first day. Now move along."

But Skink didn't move. Instead, he stood there, feet about shoulder-length apart, arms away from his sides. His eyes were no longer focused on Sammy, and they never went over to James Lee. Instead he seemed intent on a spot either directly behind Sammy or infinitely more distant.

"Skink," Sammy said again, a pleading note in his voice. Wondering if this was always going to be his role, putting his own body in place of someone else's. Getting dunked for someone else. "Skink."

"Move it, kid!" James Lee sounded a bit exasperated. This may have been the longest time anyone *hadn't* done what he told them to since first grade.

*And maybe*, Sammy thought, *James Lee was afraid of having someone defy him successfully. Because . . . because . . .* Sammy almost had it, the key to James Lee's personality.

Before Sammy could finish that thought, Skink's whole body tensed, and he inhaled loudly, causing James Lee to take an uncertain step backward. Then Skink's right hand flashed high in the air, and he shouted a loud "Kee-eye!!" and plunged his hand down almost faster than Sammy could follow, punching right *through* the table.

The Formica top shattered where he struck it, and the whole thing folded in on itself, collapsing to the floor with a horrible clatter.

James Lee couldn't seem to take his eyes off the broken table. Neither could anyone else in the suddenly graveyard-quiet lunchroom.

"I don't want to sit here anyway," Skink said without smiling. "The table's broken."

He walked away from James Lee and moved evenly toward Sammy, his shoulders squared back, head high, hands at his sides.

The lunchroom went from deathly quiet to a standing riot in about twenty seconds, little Bobby Marstall leading the yells. Sammy didn't know where to look—at Skink or James Lee or the seventh graders all of whom were clapping and high-fiving and grinning. But his attention was suddenly focused on Skink who was closing in on him.

When he was close enough to speak, Skink said quietly, "I think I might have broken my hand."

Sammy glanced down at Skink's right hand. It did look alarmingly swollen. "Let's go to the nurse!" he hissed.

Skink shook his head. "We'll eat first."

"Okay." It seemed the right thing to say. The only thing to say. Despite his obvious pain, Skink grinned. "You'll have to share your lunch." He waved his left hand at the heap that used to be a table. "Mine is somewhere under that."

Sammy chuckled uncertainly, and they walked to a table far away from the still-gawking James Lee and his crew of cretins. Walked away to a table by the door.

There was only one other person at the table, a dark-haired eighth-grade girl with a long face and a deep dimple in her cheek. Sammy had never had the courage to speak to her. She was as much a loner as he, but it didn't seem to trouble her. In fact, she wore that aloneness like a badge. Her name—he whispered it under his breath—was Julia Nathanson. It had a softness to it that he liked.

He didn't even dare ask if they could sit with her, but she nodded at them anyway, the tips of her straight hair coming together to veil her face, hiding the dimple.

"This is good," Skink said, his voice straining through the pain.

They sat down and Sammy shared what was on his

plate. They began to eat slowly, as if nothing was wrong or changed, though everything was wrong and at the same time changed beyond recognition.

Several seventh graders—Bobby Marstall and another boy and a girl Sammy didn't recognize at all—came over and tried to sit down with them, but Sammy waved them off.

"Skink needs quiet after that karate chop," he told them. "Julia stays because she was here already." He was breathless having said her name, but she gave no sign that she had even heard him.

The kids nodded, and Bobby spoke for all of them, saying, "Great karate chop, man!" Then they left, but not before Bobby whispered over his shoulder, "And thanks, Sammy."

Sammy grinned and was about to explain it to Skink, when Skink spoke first.

"Not karate," Skink said, his voice tight with pain. "It's called Hwa Rang Do."

For a minute Sammy worried that Skink's broken hand was making him feverish and that he was rambling. But then Julia repeated it.

"Not karate. Hwa Rang Do," she said to her tray.

"The Way of a Flowering Knight. It's a Korean martial art, eighteen hundred years old." Then she took the tray and left the table, dumping what was left of her lunch into the proper bins.

"She's right," Skink said. "How'd she know that?"

"I have no idea," Sammy said, hoping to stop thinking about Julia Nathanson, "Eighteen hundred years old?"

Skink nodded.

"*Whereas*," Sammy used one of his favorite words, "whereas you and I are thirteen."

"Well, actually, I'm almost fifteen. Lost a grade with all that moving."

"Well, I skipped a grade so I'm not *quite* thirteen. In the spring. My mom tutored me."

"That's quite a not quite," Skink said.

"We've moved a lot as well," Sammy told him.

"You, like, an army brat, too?"

"Nah—a pottery brat."

Skink just nodded as if he understood. And maybe he did. Or maybe it made no difference to him, and he just accepted Sammy as he was.

Julia returned and looked at them through her

hair. "It's none of my business, but I think your hand is swollen and you should do something . . ."

"I'm fine," Skink said.

"He's fine," Sammy added.

Julia shrugged. "Just saying." She turned, walked a few steps away, then shook the hair away from her face. "Are you sure?"

"Sure." They said it together, Skink's voice tight with pain and Sammy's tight with . . . well, with what he wasn't quite sure.

Julia shrugged again. "Okay then." Without saying a word more, she went straight out the door, not looking back.

"Nice girl," said Skink, his voice still controlled, like a clock too tightly wound.

"Yeah," Sammy said, trying to match that control and failing. His voice cracked as if the word had two syllables instead of one.

They were silent for some time after that, sharing the food. Skink ate clumsily with his left hand, all the while cradling his right in his lap. This gave Sammy time to consider what they should do next. At last he said, "The nurse is down the hall from here." He gestured out the cafeteria door. "I'll hold your back."

"It's my hand that hurts, not my back," Skink said.

"I'm *not* holding your hand," Sammy said. "Life is tough enough here without . . ."

"That's a *joke*, Samson," Skink said, and got to his feet without help. "I think I'll skip the nurse and go straight home. My dad always says 'Go to a Nurse, Send for the Hearse.'"

"That's an odd saying."

"The major's an odd man," Skink replied, and walked into the hall.

Sammy blinked at his back, then got up and quickly followed. "You call your dad 'the major'?"

"Not, like, to his face."

Sammy pulled a cell phone out of his backpack. "What's your home number?"

"Awesome," said Skink. "My parents won't let me have a cell."

Sammy shrugged. "My parents won't let me go anywhere *without* one. Not since the day I came home from here with a black eye."

Skink looked at him under drooping eyelids. Sammy suspected that was because of the pain. "When was that?"

"The second day of eighth grade. And now it's nearly Thanksgiving break. Lots of fun's been had by all in such a short time." It came out much more bitterly than he meant.

Skink gave him the number, and Sammy dialed, then handed the phone to his friend. *Friend.* The word seemed odd here in the halls of Madison Junior/Senior High School where friends had been pretty thin on the ground. Sammy rolled the word around in his mouth, which is what he liked to do with any word he especially liked. *Friend.*

After speaking a few sentences in hushed, tight tones, Skink handed the phone back. "The major's coming to get me."

"Does it hurt badly? Your hand?"

Skink lifted his right hand up with his left. They both looked at it. It was clearly swollen and a bit bruised looking at the knuckles, though with Skink's dark skin that was hard to tell. Skink wiggled his fingers tentatively. "Maybe not actually broken."

"That would be good."

"That would be, like, *excellent.*" Skink's face lit up as if pain were only a memory. "I'm a guitar player. Well, actually, I'm learning to play."

Sammy started grinning like a manic Halloween pumpkin. "I play music, too."

"Guitar?"

"No—clarinet."

"Get out."

"Only Madison has no school band."

"That's all right. I wouldn't want to play music with this bunch," Skink said. "Imagine what James Lee would play."

Sammy tried. "Drums? He's good at banging on things."

"Nah," said Skink. "He's a triangle man. Makes a lot of high-pitched noise but really says nothing."

"He's a blowhard." Sammy said.

"What's that, Word Man?" asked Skink.

"It means someone who brags more than he performs."

"*Blowhard!* He is indeed. I like your word." Skink puffed up his cheeks and then blew hard as if trying to douse a cake full of burning candles.

For a moment they both held back the laugh and then it burst from them as if from an uncapped fire hydrant. And when they finished laughing, they stared at one another, each waiting for the other to make the offer. Their friendship was too new to be compromised by saying the wrong thing.

At last, Sammy took the plunge. He could feel his heart stuttering in his chest. "We could . . ."

And Skink jumped in with him. "We could start a *band*."

They looked at one another and grinned.

"A band!" they said together, both so excited by the prospect, that without thinking, Skink thrust his right hand into the air in a fist and ended up screaming with pain.

That scream made two things happened at the same time. Mrs. Murphy, the school secretary, dyed red hair curling in tendrils around her reddened cheeks, rushed out of her office and started to scold them both. And the outside door opened. A tall black man with impossibly broad shoulders stomped in.

"Skinner John Williams," both the secretary and the man said together, and Skink immediately snapped to attention, turning toward his father.

"What did you do to yourself, son?" asked Major Williams. The words were soft but the voice was huge.

Skink held up his hand.

"Broken?" his father asked in his loud voice.

"Did you show the nurse?" Mrs. Murphy asked at the same time.

"Nurse to hearse," Major Williams snapped. "Madam, I'm taking my son to the doctor ASAP." It was a statement, not a question.

*ASAP.* It was a new word for Sammy and he liked it. "ASAP?" he whispered to Skink.

"Army speak for *as soon as possible.* Like right now."

Major Williams put a hand on Skink's shoulder, nodded at Sammy, and said loudly, "I assume you were a help to my boy."

Sammy nodded back, unable to speak, all the words he knew suddenly sticking in his throat.

The bell rang.

"Time for class, Sammy," Mrs. Murphy said.

"Skinner John!" the big voice boomed, as the major turned smartly to the right and headed for the door.

"See you, like, tomorrow, Samson," Skink said. "Stay out of the bathroom till then."

And then they were gone.

Sammy stared after Skink thinking that it had been a very strange day, a two-rescue day. With a swim in the porcelain pool in-between.

Suddenly, the bell rang again, loud and angry.

Mrs. Murphy said, "You're tardy now, Sammy!"

*Again.*

Sammy sighed and ran off to class.

Aside from another scolding for being late to class, the rest of the school day passed uneventfully. Even the bus ride home was peaceful. Not for a moment did Sammy think his tormentors had stopped for good, but Skink's display had certainly given them pause. *And what a pause!* Sammy was able to lean his head back and close his eyes on the bus for the first time for . . . well, forever. He wouldn't need saving by Mr. Baer. Not today. In fact, the entire bus was noticeably subdued.

When Sammy got off, he had an uncharacteristic spring to his step on the two-block walk home.

Home was a ugly stucco house, drab brown and unassuming in design but with a lot of room inside. It sat on a nine-acre plot that ended down at the Mill River, a lazy serpentine run of water that should have had large trout in it but didn't.

Mom called the house a *tardis* after the *Doctor Who* TV show, which was the only one she'd actually watched before selling their TV set—a *tardis* being something that looked small on the outside but contained universes within. It had two floors, which included a full basement. But what really sold them on the house had been the three-car garage. Sammy's dad had immediately converted it into a pottery studio, leaving the family's beat-up minivan to sit sulking in the driveway.

Sammy shrugged as his street came into view. His parents might be weirder than most parents but it didn't faze him anymore. He had darker forces to fight in school.

"Like the Marching Morons," he whispered.

When Sammy got within half a block of the safety of home, he saw his dad standing beside the car in a mud-spattered apron. Hands on his hips, he was leaning backward to stretch his spine. Sammy knew he'd probably spent all day sitting at the wheel until "the potter's stool has to get surgically removed from his butt," as Mom liked to say. But his dad was also watching Sammy's return in case the Boyz—as he dubbed them—

had trailed Sammy home. It had happened before. Not once, but several times.

Sammy's dad was short and stocky with big, Popeye-looking arms from long hours throwing clay. Pottery was not just his business but his passion. Sammy couldn't remember a time when his dad wasn't covered with bits of clay. His hair was thinning in front but remained thick, curly, and wild in back, and he wore thin-rimmed glasses that would have given him the look of a college professor if they hadn't been heavily speckled with bits of gray clay, as if they had some sort of disease.

"Clay pox," Mom called it.

"Father, I am home," Sammy's voice was strange, deep, formal, not at all his school voice, which was high and often desperate sounding, like the voice of a cornered mouse.

Dad broke out of his stretch and fixed Sammy with eyes that glinted with humor. He answered with equally deep formality. "And have you made your fortune, Son?"

"Not today, Father." It was an old game they played, ever since Sammy had been about three years old, because of their shared love of fairy tales.

Dad sighed theatrically, breath frosting in the cold air. "I'll have to keep working, then. Someone has to

keep this family afloat. And you'd better get started on
your homework."

"Not yet, Dad," Sammy said. "I need to practice
clarinet first!"

"Imagine that. You're going to delay homework to
play music. Shocking!"

*Sometimes*, Sammy thought, *Dad's attempts at humor
are pretty lame.*

Scampering into the house and shucking his coat,
shoes, and backpack inside the front door, Sammy
went straight to the basement. With Dad's studio in
the garage, the basement had been freed up as a rec
room, and Sammy had taken it over. He walked past
bookshelves stuffed so full that any new books couldn't
actually be shelved but had to sit on top in piles. His
mother liked to say, "It's lucky Sammy's books have
been moved to the basement or the house might have
fallen in on itself."

He headed straight for the "Music Area," though
that was a rather lofty title for the corner of the basement
that contained Sammy's clarinet, a folding chair, a
music stand holding staff paper, a precariously perched
metronome, and—of course—a small bookshelf. But
instead of fairy tales, fantasy novels, and young adult

adventures (his usual reading choices) this shelf held only music books. And not just *any* music books. These were *klezmer* music books.

Sammy had begun music lessons studying classical clarinet in third grade. By sixth grade he was in the school band, playing pop music and marching songs. But when his grandfather had sent him several CDs of klezmer music for his birthday, Sammy had been hooked. And now he was learning to play klezmer, the folk/pop music of the Jewish people. His uncle Freddy, a real professional musician, had told him lots of stuff about *klez*, as he called it, at a family bar mitzvah before Sammy's dad had hauled them all to the Midwest in his quest for a cheap studio. Uncle Freddy said klez was a mishmash of styles that shouldn't work but did—a sound perfect for a people who were spread all over the world, but still shared a religion, a culture, a music.

"The original fusion music," said Uncle Freddy.

In fact, Sammy couldn't remember a time he hadn't been in love with those slinky, gliding melodies, the polka backbeat, the jazz chords, the New Orleans horns. So while other kids listened to soft rock or hip-hop or country—depending on which school clique they were in—Sammy listened to bands like the Klezmatics and

Brave Old World. He even had a sticker on his clarinet case that read: DRUNK ON KLEZMER JUICE, which Uncle Freddy had given him the day they moved.

When his parents had first realized how passionate Sammy was about the music, they'd given in.

"Which instrument?" Mom had asked hesitantly.

His father added, "We can't afford a piano . . . not yet, son."

Sammy had grinned and didn't hesitate. "Clarinet."

Clarinet was the voice of klezmer.

Pulling his clarinet case out, he sat down on the chair. Putting the instrument together was a ritual. Wet the reed, check the cork. Push the bell, joints, and barrel together, pushing as you go, then the ligature and reed get strapped on like a toreador's belt before he goes to face the bull. Lifting the clarinet to his lips, he licked the reed a couple times, blew a note, then adjusted his *embouchure*—the way his mouth held the instrument. With his top teeth touching the reed less firmly than before—he had a tendency to bite when he played his first note of the day, something that his old teacher had *nearly* cured him of—he blew a second note, strong and clean.

Then came the scales. Major first, then minors, to warm up. Then the fun ones. The klezmer ones: *Ahava Raba*, with its flat second and raised third, and *Mi Sheberach*, the altered Dorian mode. He knew he should do more, but Sammy was impatient to play some tunes.

Klezmer is dance music. That was the very first thing he learned about it. Uncle Freddy said it every time they met. And though he sat down to assemble the clarinet and stayed sitting to run the scales, Sammy always stood up to play so he could sort of be dancing, too. He was weaving back and forth, the tip of his clarinet dancing little circles and figure eights in the air, as he blew a Bulgar circle dance. He'd never played Klez with anyone except for his old clarinet teacher, but in his head he could hear a bass *oom-pah*-ing, as well as a piano mimicking it, and an accordion doubling the melody with him.

He switched to a *kolomeike*, fast and furious, and his imaginary band switched as well. Then he was on his own, playing a mournful introduction to the next piece.

*But maybe not alone for much longer.* Soon the imaginary band he jammed with would be replaced by one real friend.

Then Sammy stopped thinking and simply lost

himself in the music until his mother came home from her work at the local library and called him up to dinner. He'd been so engrossed in playing, he hadn't even noticed the time or the smell of the food cooking in the kitchen.

At dinner, the family got right down to the ritual of eating. Mom always called it the "Greenburg Grabfast." Not a word was allowed till after they'd all had at least seven bites.

*Seven!* Sammy never knew where that rule had come from, but they kept it religiously. It was the only religion they actually practiced. Well, until that very moment. He ate his seven bites quickly, then looked up brightly, ready to point out that he'd finished.

His mother was waving a piece of paper at them.

Dad had a hand up to stop her as he was finishing his seventh bite. Then he smiled in her direction.

Sammy knew the letter. It was from Grandpa Aron, the only person in the universe who wasn't online.

"Grandpa writes that he'll pay for a bar mitzvah if we can find a Hebrew teacher somewhere close by. And I've managed to find a rabbi *and* a synagogue." She smiled encouragingly in Sammy's direction.

Sammy glared at her and his dad, who said nothing, which was odd because he was not one to be quiet about religious matters.

"Not easy to find out this way," Mom said. "It's in Carston. An hour from here." She waved her hand vaguely toward the north, though Sammy—who liked to read maps—knew the town was really southwest from there.

"But, Mom . . ." Sammy had said before she raised a warning hand.

"You know Grandpa Aron isn't well and, as you're his only grandson, and named after his father, we can't really say no, can we?"

There wasn't any need to argue. It was a done deed—finished, sealed, stamped, delivered. *Just like that letter,* Sammy thought. Once his mother made up her mind about something, there was no going back. *So now I have to be driven fifty miles to learn an unlearnable language in order to have a party when I turn thirteen that no one here will come to.*

Feeling grumbly, he decided to tackle another seven

bites just so he didn't snap at his mother and father and get detention at home as well. Normally he loved his mom's spaghetti and meatballs, but her announcement had taken away his appetite, maybe forever. After his third bite—two of the meatballs and one of the spaghetti—he put his fork down.

Mom looked long and hard at him. "Don't forget your greens. You know, they won't poison you."

Sammy made a face. "You should have said that before . . ." Then he put his right hand on his neck and stuck out his tongue as if he'd really been poisoned.

To delay the actual green deed, he shoveled some of the limp spinach carefully onto his fork. He had an announcement of his own, and it might just change everything. Casually, he said, "I made a friend today." He didn't mention sitting with Julia Nathanson. That was too new and too personal to tell anyone, especially his parents.

"A friend," Mom said, smiling. "How nice." She didn't elaborate, in case this was Sammy's idea of a joke. Or an end run around the bar mitzvah news. Sammy knew she was brilliant that way, figuring out every angle. She had a degree in child psychology, not that she could find a job here in that field.

"Someone to bring home some time?" Dad asked. His voice was neutral on purpose, like a car at a stop sign.

Swallowing the mouthful of the hated greens, Sammy nodded.

"Good." Dad looked down at the spaghetti and meatballs on his plate and grated himself a little mountain of Parmesan over the top.

Mom stared at them both. "*Good* is all you can say? It's Sammy's first friend since we got here. Four months, since July, and then that nastiness at school with those boys, and that's all you can say? *Good?* It's *wonderful*, Sammy." Obviously she'd made up her mind that Sammy hadn't made a joke and was going all out. "What's his name?"

Sammy was about to say, "How do you know it isn't a her?" But instead he finished swallowing. Hesitated a beat. Then said quietly, "Skink." He waited for their reaction. It was not long in coming.

"SKINK?" They said it together, like some kind of comedy act.

Mom added, "I hope that's a nickname."

At the same time Dad said, "Of course that's a nickname."

Sammy sighed. "His whole name is Skinner John

Williams. He's named after his grandfathers. But everyone calls him Skink."

*This is worse*, Sammy thought, *than being grilled by the CIA*. But by dinner's end, some forty-eight bites later (Sammy knew because he was counting every one of them), his mother said, "Why not ask Skink for dinner, Sammy. For Sunday."

Getting up from the table to help put the dishes in the washer, Dad added, "We'd love to meet him."

*They've* got *to be kidding*.

Standing to do his part of the cleanup—the glasses and silverware—Sammy thought about that invitation. There was no way he would ever—*ever*—ask Skink to meet his parents. He wouldn't want anyone to have to sit through that kind of grilling.

Especially not a new friend.

A new friend who could split Formica tabletops with his bare hand.

But on Sunday, when the doorbell rang and Sammy went to answer it, he was thinking, *I never should have told them his real name.*

His mother hadn't waited for Sammy to invite Skink; she called his parents herself. It turned out, Mrs.

Williams wanted to come over right away, to thank Sammy for all he'd done. And she wouldn't think of making Mrs. Greenburg cook. She and Major Williams hadn't had a grown-up date night in ages, so busy with their moving. They'd take the opportunity to go out. The two moms had had a lovefest over the phone. Or at least so it seemed from what Sammy overheard. Sammy could only imagine what it had sounded like from the other side. Skink would probably never forgive him.

Opening the door, Sammy was ready to apologize for his mother, indeed for Jewish mothers everywhere.

Skink and his father stood on the doorstep.

"I have to . . ." Sammy started.

"Hey, Sammy." Skink stepped in, punching Sammy lightly on the arm with his right hand. The hand he had hurt. He held a guitar case in his left.

"Good evening, Samson," said Major Williams loudly, enveloping Sammy in a painfully firm handshake before walking past. Only then was his wife revealed—a thin but quite tall Asian woman who'd been hidden by his bulk. He turned slightly and spoke to her, even more loudly than before. "Jin, this is the boy we told you about. Samson."

"I'm called Sammy," Sammy began.

"Samson's a man's name! A strong man!" the major said in his large voice, indicating by its very loudness that Sammy was going to be Samson to him forever.

"Hello, Sammy," said Skink's mom. Her handshake was mercifully gentler than her husband's. "John has told me so much about you." She had a light accent.

"John?" Sammy asked.

"She's never approved of *Skinner* as a name," Major Williams roared in his parade-ground voice. "But a family name's no shame, I always say," going on loud enough that Sammy was sure the neighbors could hear, though there weren't any closer than a football field away. "Be proud of your name, son. It's a Biblical name. A strong man's name. As you were when you took care of Skinner in the face of an overwhelming enemy. Now, where's the head of the household? Ah, there she is." His voice never lowered the entire time.

Sammy's mom was just walking in, drying her hands on her apron. His dad came right behind, cleaned up with nary a clay spot on him, Sammy was relieved to note. There were more handshakes plus introductions all around.

"I like a man with a strong handshake," the major said to Sammy's dad.

"Throwing pots all day long will do that," Sammy's dad answered in an equally large voice, as if suddenly competing in the "loud father" match.

"Pots? Pots?" Mrs. Williams stepped forward saying, "My grandfather was a well-known potter in Korea. He said there were potters in the family going back to the Three Kingdoms."

"We have pottery all over the house. A man has to be careful swinging a stick . . ." Major Williams said, still without moderating his voice, but he smiled when he said it.

They walked into the living room, and Mrs. Williams went right over to the cabinet with the pots. "I see, I see. You are very talented. Do you take inspiration from the Korean?"

Sammy's dad nodded. "The celadon especially, it is my homage to the Korean masters."

She bent closer to the glass. "Yes, yes, I see that. You have the simplicity."

Sammy was astonished. In just a few moments, Mrs. Williams knew more about his dad's work than Sammy had learned in almost thirteen years.

"Say—there was a Greenburg in my unit in the first Gulf War," Major Williams boomed. "He was five foot nothing and a hundred pounds, rifle included. Toughest soldier I ever saw. Any kin to you?" His voice seemed to echo off the walls.

Sammy's dad smiled. "They don't usually make us Jews real big, that's true."

"Excepting Samson. In the Bible," Major Williams said, the walls echoing.

"Excepting Samson," Sammy's dad agreed, though much more quietly. "But no close kin of mine was in the Gulf War. And Greenburg's a pretty popular name among European Jews."

"We lived for a while in Israel," said the major. "Jin and I. When we were first married. I was teaching in the war college. Before Skinner came along."

Mrs. Williams said, "We Koreans are rarely made this tall, either. But, dear," and she turned to the major, "we have a six-thirty reservation. We need to go ASAP."

The major seemed to snap to attention. "Ah, yes." If anything, his voice had become louder. "At Shim Chung's. Finest Asian fusion in . . ."

The grown-ups went back to the door, and Sammy shrugged at Skink who shrugged right back. A knowing look passed between them that said it all, all anyone his age felt about having embarrassing parents.

"Basement," Sammy said, pointing to the door that led to the stairs. "Music room."

And down they went.

At the bottom of the stairs, Sammy turned around, closing the door behind them—quietly, but with a grateful finality.

"Whew."

"So," Skink breathed, and then followed with the best possible thing he could have said ever, "what kind of, like, band are we going to have?"

Sammy didn't hesitate. "Klezmer."

"Klezmer?" Skink said, tilting his head to the side. "Where have I heard of that?"

"It's Jewish music," Sammy said. "Your dad said they lived in Israel before you were born. Maybe they got some CDs there?"

Nodding, Skink said, "Yeah. That's probably it. Not sure if I've listened to much. What's it like?"

"Kind of like jazz."

"I like jazz."

"And kind of like folk music."

Skink scrunched up his eyebrows. "Not so sure about folk."

"And it's kind of like . . ." Sammy wasn't sure how to describe Klezmer. Nobody had ever been interested before. As soon as he said "Jewish music" the conversation was usually over. "Let me play you some."

"Oh—okay."

Sammy ran to the CD shelves that lined the music area.

*Could put on* Perlman Plays Klezmer. *Can't beat Itzhak Perlman for pure musicianship. But it might be a little square for someone who likes jazz. And I really want him to love klez.* Sammy pondered his choices for another moment. Then he snapped his fingers. *Got it!*

He grabbed a CD from the rack and held it up. "The Klezmatics!"

"Okay," Skink said noncommittally. "What's it called?"

"Jews with Horns." Sammy grinned.

Skink scratched a spot just over his left temple. "Didn't people used to think Jewish people had horns?" Then he grinned back. "Oh—I get it." The horns section of the Klezmatics had just kicked in.

*I like this guy!* Sammy thought. *A smart friend.*

Sammy did end up playing Skink some Itzhak Perlman as well. He also played him Klezmorim and Streimel and Brave Old World and all the best tracks from his best CDs.

Finally, after a half hour of listening, Skink spoke up, saying simply: "I like it."

"Excellent," Sammy said. "Let's . . ."

"But," Skink interrupted, "I think we should play more than just Klezmer."

It wasn't something Sammy had ever considered. "Why?"

Skink frowned. "Well, it kind of limits our audience."

"I suppose it does." He grinned. "You don't think James Lee is a closet Klez-maniac?"

"'Fraid not!" Skink said. "But since you, like, love the music, let's learn us some Klez." He bent to open his guitar case. "But then let me teach you some jazz. And some funk. And maybe just a little bit of rock."

"Rock the clarinet?" Sammy asked uncertainly.

Skink grinned at him. "You'll certainly get points for originality."

*And points*, Sammy thought, *for interesting friends.*

Skink took his guitar out of its case and began to tune it. His hand seemed entirely healed.

"Doesn't it hurt even a little?" Sammy asked,

pointing to the hand and remembering how swollen it had looked just days earlier.

"Nope. I'm like my dad. My body gets better almost instantly. It's—like—a gift. That's why No Nurse . . ." He began to let his fingers run up and down the strings.

"Maybe you're an alien."

"I am."

Sammy's mouth dropped open. At this point, he was ready to believe anything.

"I was born in Korea. But not to worry. I have an American passport as well. Won't be able to become president of the United States, though."

Sammy nodded, oddly relieved and yet oddly disappointed about the alien thing. *I mean, if he'd actually come from Mars . . . how cool would that be?* But as Skink ran some small riffs, Sammy stopped worrying and really started to listen. Finally, he picked up his clarinet, moistening the reed with his tongue.

He thought about the way Skink was riffing. Not a real tune but just noodling around, playing with the klez tunes they'd been listening to for the past thirty minutes.

*Skink's really good*, he thought. *Not just good for an almost fifteen-year-old. Good-good!*

Sammy listened some more till an idea came to

him. He gave his clarinet a few tentative honks and then swung in.

Skink immediately switched to fuller voicings for his chords, providing a deep background of notes for Sammy to soar over. Sammy dipped and dived around the chords, and when he threatened to touch bottom, Skink dove up the neck of his guitar and rattled off a few high runs while Sammy oompahed a faux bass line on the clarinet.

They went on like this for Sammy didn't know how long, trading licks and exploring rhythms till Sammy went for a note and missed and produced one of those squeaky, creaky squeals that only a clarinet can do, and they both burst out laughing.

"Is that klez—or even close?" Skink asked.

"Are you Jewish or even close?" Sammy asked. "Seriously, it might not be real klez, but I really like the other styles you were throwing in. Why can't we be a klezmer fusion garage band?"

"Because," Skink said, affecting a deep drawl, "we ain't in no garage."

That started them laughing again.

"Seriously . . ." Skink said, taking a deep breath, "that's a rowser of an idea. Klezmer. Fusion. Garage. Band."

"But there's only two of us. Not much of a band," Sammy said. "More like a duo."

"Exactly like a duo," said Skink. His nose crinkled as if he were smelling something bad.

More laughter ensued, threatening to turn into more giggles.

"Maybe we could get one of James Lee's crew to drum for us," said Skink. "They like to bang on things."

"And think of all the drummer jokes we could tell," Sammy said. "How do you know if the stage is level?"

"The drummer drools out of both sides of his mouth," Skink said. "How do you confuse a drummer?"

"Put a sheet of music in front of him."

They broke out into hysterics all over again. Finally—and simultaneously—in an attempt to be serious, they began to play, up and down minor scales, in and out of songs they each knew and some that they both knew, trying to give each a wailing klezmer sound.

Sammy had never been happier. To have a friend. To have a friend who plays music. To have a friend who wants to be in a band. Well, a duo anyway. All the past— the bullying, the dunkings in the toilet, the spitting in his food, the not-so-subtle trippings as he walked down the school hallway—even the black eye—he let go. Or rather he put it into his mouth and blew it through the clarinet, until it was gone.

They played for two hours, maybe three, never keeping track of the time. And then a drum started. A series of rat-a-tats. A loud taradiddle.

A drum?

There was no drum. They had no drummer.

Only then did Sammy realize that someone was knocking on the basement door. He stopped playing and slowly Skink stopped playing, too. They both looked expectantly toward the door.

"All right, boys, we've finished our meal and are back, and the general says it's time to go." The major's stentorian voice boomed through the door.

Sammy turned to Skink, and mouthed, "The *general?*"

Skink was already slipping out of the guitar strap and bending over the case to put the instrument away. "That's what he calls my mom."

"Oh." Sammy put the clarinet on the music stand.

Skink smiled. "But not, like, to her face."

At the door, they all shook hands, smiling, the grown-ups speaking adult pleasantries.

"See you tomorrow," Skink said.

*Tomorrow,* Sammy thought. *I'll see my* friend *tomorrow. In school.*

That's when he remembered all the bad stuff that school had on offer. And he knew as surely as he knew the sun was coming up in the morning that the bad stuff would start all over again. Probably be worse. But at least this time he had a friend to share it with.

Monday morning bus ride, no problems. Ditto for morning classes. At lunch Skink and Sammy brainstormed names for their band.

"Could name it Van Halen," Skink suggested.

"How do you mean?"

Skink put his fork down and flashed his hands out in front of him, exclaiming, "Greenburg!"

Sammy frowned. "Too Jewish."

"Skink!"

"Not Jewish enough."

"Metalliklez?"

"Too weird."

"Well," Skink said with a sigh, "do you have any, like, suggestions?"

"Not really. I'm still thinking." Staring down at his tray, he added, "Mostly about what they were trying to do when they cooked this meat, whatever it is."

Skink shoveled a forkful into his mouth. "I learned a long time ago to not ask those kinds of questions," he said, chewing, a lot of his consonants lost in the mush. Enough survived for Sammy to catch the sentence's meaning. "Army food, you know."

"*You* weren't in the army. Your dad was."

"Yeah. And sometimes he decides to cook." Skink shuddered at the memory. "But enough about food—we need to name our band."

Sammy poked at the lump on his plate, not quite ready to eat until he'd positively identified it. "What we need are more band members and—that way—more ideas."

"That, too." Skink scooped up some more food. "I might know someone."

"Chicken," Sammy said. "I'm *pretty* sure it's chicken. Well, *almost* sure." He closed his eyes and took a bite. All he tasted was salt. He decided that was probably not a bad thing. "Who do you know?"

"Julia Nathanson."

Sammy almost choked on his almost-sure chicken.

"Julia?" His heart skipped a beat. Either that, or the chicken had tap-danced on it.

"Yeah, the girl who sat with us on Friday. Remember her?"

*Only all night long since Friday. Only all weekend long.* Sammy didn't say it aloud. Not even to Skink. Skink might laugh. He might say something snotty. *He might*— and here Sammy sighed, then quickly covered it with a cough—*Skink might even—like—like her.*

"She's in my homeroom. I called her to thank her for her concern and asked how she knew about Hwa Rang Do. Turns out she knows lots of cool stuff. And she, like, plays fiddle."

"Fiddle!" Now Sammy's heart was beating overtime. He couldn't tell if it was because he was mad that Skink had called Julia, or glad. "Do you think . . ."

"I can ask," Skink said.

"*I* can ask," Sammy said.

Skink grinned. "Okay. It's your band."

"Naw," Sammy said, "it's ours."

And they would have asked her together only Julia wasn't in the lunchroom. In fact, she wasn't in school that day.

Julia didn't come to school the next day or the next either, which was just as well because the Boyz were back to bashing on Sammy. Before Julia had inserted herself into his life, it hadn't mattered who knew how often he was picked on. And now, somehow, it did.

He supposed the renewed bashing had to do with his own big mouth. Sammy couldn't help it. He said something snotty to the Boyz, and in return they knocked the snot out of him. Then he said something even snottier. It had become an endurance contest, though he was the only one doing the enduring. But if Julia had known about the bashings, Sammy suddenly knew that everything would have been worse. A disaster. An embarrassment. The end of his particular world. Of this Sammy was absolutely sure.

So while Sammy wondered why she was absent—family crisis, the flu, a change of schools, possibly a move to another state, time travel, abduction by aliens—he was actually relieved.

Of course, James Lee didn't care about any of that. All he cared about was cornering Sammy. Cornering Sammy without Skink around. Because it had become clear to Sammy that James Lee was not about to face Skink down. Not yet. Not till he figured out Skink's weaknesses.

"That's it!" Sammy said aloud as he walked down the hall between classes. He finally understood the main thing about James Lee. He wasn't good at schoolwork. He couldn't remember anything about English or civics or math. But he has a positive genius—*like a predator*, Sammy thought—for finding someone's weak spot and poking it hard.

Sammy's weak spot was that he didn't—couldn't— fight back with his fists, which seemed to be the only kind of fighting James Lee considered worthy, because he was deathly afraid of being hit in the mouth and ruining his embouchure forever, meaning he might never be able to play clarinet again. So he did everything possible to get out of fighting James Lee and his crew, except he couldn't seem to shut up when cornered by them. Or when the Boyz threatened someone smaller. Which meant—he shuddered—one of these days fist and mouth were bound to connect.

But as for Skink, James Lee didn't know his weak spot yet. Sammy hoped he didn't have one. Because if he did, James Lee was sure to find it.

Sammy spent the three days Julia was absent skulking around corners. He was late for every class, just making sure he didn't run into James Lee, which meant he had three days worth of after-school detentions to serve.

He played sick for one period on Monday just so he could use the bathroom off the principal's office. Another time he sneaked out of the school and peed in the bushes. Yes, he was scared that someone might see him and call him a pervert or something. But he didn't care, as long as he was safe from another dunking in the toilet.

And his sneaking worked for two days.

*Two whole days!* It seemed a vacation, a heaven, an eternity.

He and Skink only had gym class together. Since that was a class without James Lee, it was the one time he could relax.

*Perhaps*, he thought, *I've relaxed a bit too much.* For in the middle of a fast-paced dodgeball game, the big red ball hit him on the side of the head. Not near his mouth, thank goodness. But close to his right eye. He didn't exactly see stars. They were more like half notes. He shook his head to clear it.

"Hey, sorry," Bobby Marstall called out. He'd been the thrower and, for once, accurate.

"Nothing broken," Sammy yelled back, "except my pride. And I've got plenty more of that."

Everyone in the gym class laughed, and Sammy— liking the sound of it— laughed with them.

Skink pounded him on the back. "Careful with that mouth," he whispered, and it wasn't clear if he meant that Sammy shouldn't mouth off, or if he was worried about Sammy being able to play the clarinet.

"No problemo," Sammy said, meaning both.

Either way, Sammy was glad he had a friend who cared.

Both days he and Skink sat down together at an empty table that quickly filled up with seventh and eighth graders. *Safety in numbers*, Sammy thought gratefully, though he knew the others weren't there to save him but to talk to Skink. But Skink often deferred to Sammy.

"Hey, Skink, where'd you learn those karate moves?" Bobby Marstall asked, making a chopping motion with his right hand while his left pushed his glasses back up the bridge of his nose.

Mouth full, Skink gestured to Sammy.

"It's not karate," Sammy said quickly. "It's a Korean martial arts. Over a thousand years old. He's been studying it for some time."

"Though not a thousand years, I bet!" That was Marsha Hazelton. She looked around expecting a patter of laughter, and there was a little.

Sammy nodded, adding, "Skink's mom is Korean and she's got great moves, too. A black belt. She's known throughout Korea. In fact, she's amazing." Now Sammy was just making stuff up, but Skink seemed to enjoy it. "His mom was born in Seoul, which is the capital of Korea, which makes Skink a soul man in two ways."

For a moment there was a blank look around the table, and then Bobby brightened. "Oh, like soul food. And . . . er . . ." Now laughter pounded the table and Sammy glanced to the right where James Lee and his gang were at another table, not even eating, just watching. They were too far away to have heard any of the actual conversation, but their reaction to the laughter was one of scowls and rapid-fire glares, as if they assumed the laughter was at their expense.

Sammy realized there was a battle brewing, but for

the first time he felt he was holding his own. He had a champion in Skink, and a table full of friends.

But James Lee suddenly began to stand up, unfolding in a loose, almost boneless way, like something out of a monster movie.

"Attack of the skin men," Sammy whispered, nodding in James Lee's direction.

Still chewing, Skink flexed his hands. It was clear from his expression that the right hand was still sore.

Sammy imitated him, then looked around the table to see if anyone was noticing. All he saw was a sea of scared faces.

As James Lee walked toward them, his crew followed in his wake. *An armada of know-nothings*, Sammy thought. They'd been studying the Spanish Armada in history class.

James Lee planted himself at the head of Sammy's table. He was smiling lazily, like Dirty Harry on a slow day.

"Not laughing at us, I'm sure," he drawled.

"Why?" Skink said. "Are you funny?"

"Or just funny looking?" Bobby Marstall said, from the safety of the far end of the table. His face was almost green with fear. He'd clearly spoken without thinking.

Sammy swallowed visibly. He was the one closest to James Lee. He wondered if he'd be punished for what Bobby had said.

Suddenly, the James Lee crew began to surround the table, and the boys and girls all started bailing out, like rats over the side of a soon-to-be-sinking ship, leaving Skink and Sammy to face the trouble alone. There was a clattering of trays as they went, and some stuff even spilled onto the floor, but no one stopped to pick anything up.

"Now, James—" Sammy began, in what he often thought of as his apology voice, a bit whiny and higher than usual. But he never got a chance to finish because just then James Lee took a swing at Skink.

It was a big looping punch that Sammy thought would have probably knocked Skink's head clean off his shoulders if it had connected. But Skink had obviously not been as surprised as Sammy by James Lee's assault. He leaned back so that the fist whistled past his chin, assisted by a left-handed slap to the forearm that Skink delivered with the swiftness of a cobra. Then Skink was on his feet, his right hand flashing forward—holding a milk carton that smacked James Lee in the face.

Sammy was expecting the fight to be like the movies,

where every blow was accompanied by a bass thump and crack, and the action was smoothly choreographed. Instead, Skink's milk carton slap sounded like a piece of uncooked pizza dropped on a countertop. It made Sammy's stomach flip over. Blood exploded from James Lee's nose, mixing with the milk and making a crazy, starless American flag down his white T-shirt. And then Skink went down in a rush of bodies as the rest of the Boyz tackled him high and low.

Sammy had no idea what he would do once he reached his feet—run, yell, scream, kick, jump in?

*What is that reflex called? Fight or flight?* he thought wildly. But by then it didn't matter anyway. James Lee knocked the breath out of him with a casual left-handed punch before leaping on top of the writhing pile that Skink lay under.

The action got very hard to follow after that because Sammy was curled up and gasping for breath, trying desperately not to cry. Only he couldn't convince his traitor eyes not to leak.

The whole thing didn't last very long. Only long enough for teachers to appear from everywhere and start dragging kids from the pile.

At first, the Boyz threw them off and tried to get back to kicking Skink, but he was already on his feet in an instant and glaring at them, Ms. Holsten restraining him ineffectually. The Boyz probably would have tried the kicking anyway, but the wrestling coach had arrived by then and wrapped James Lee up in his massive arms. With their leader caught, the Boyz lost interest and let themselves be led quietly out of the cafeteria.

Though James Lee's nose was flattened to one side, and the wrestling coach had him in a hold that threatened to make his arms trade places with each other, he was grinning like he'd just found a hundred-dollar bill on the ground.

*Or*, Sammy thought, *like he'd just found somebody's weak spot.*

"You okay, Sammy?" asked Mrs. Henke, one of the old lunch ladies who slopped food onto the kids' trays five times a week.

"Yes," he croaked. "Wind . . . knocked . . . out."

"Well, dearie, let me help you up." Mrs. Henke put her big arms around him and hauled him to his feet. Her arms smelled like baking bread.

*Great. Everyone else is physically restrained by wrestling coaches and burly gym teachers, and I get hugged by Hilde*

*Henke. I'm sure that'll do great things for what's left of my*
*reputation.*

Still, he let himself be bundled off to the nurse's
office for a humiliating checkup ("Were you hit in the
stomach? Or someplace lower?") before being taken to
the principal's office to hear the last part of Principal
Kraft's speech, where he informed everyone involved
that if there was a repeat of this incident, suspensions
would be handed down.

"Now, I'm giving you all a week's worth of detention,"
said Principal Kraft—the Head Cheese, they all called
him, even the teachers. "And it starts now. This instant.
You'll miss the rest of the school day. All of you. Ms.
Snyder! Get them out of here. I can't stand to look at
them."

"Yeah, well, we can't stand to look at you either,
Stinky Cheese Man," said James Lee, not under his
breath enough.

"My, my," Principal Kraft said, "I do believe James
Lee you've made a book reference. Maybe school's not
entirely lost on you after all."

Sammy was more than a little astonished. And then
he thought: *Probably the teacher read the book to the class in*
*elementary school.*

He was about to say that aloud when Skink elbowed him, causing him to cough.

"Do you have something to add, Mr. Greenburg?" the principal asked.

"Nothing, sir," Sammy said quickly, and they all left the office.

"The Bug speaks," James Lee said out of the side of his mouth.

"The Stink Bug speaks," added one of his crew, a tall skinny boy with acne like pepperoni pizza.

Ms. Snyder snapped, "I heard that, Jamison Lee. And you, too, Mel Gravel."

*Jamison.* Sammy felt happy about James Lee for the first time in days. It was like all the fantasy books he'd ever read. If you know your enemy's True Name, you have power over him. He wondered if *Jamison* had ever read a book about that!

"Are you laughing, Stink Bug?" James—Jamison— Lee hissed.

"Why, Jamison?" Sammy asked as Ms. Snyder separated the boys into two groups. He finished his sentence over his shoulder as James Lee and three of his boys were stashed in the first detention room, his voice consciously mimicking Skink's. "Are you funny?"

Then he, Skink, and the shortest member of James Lee's crew, who wasn't all that short really, were herded into the second room, across the hallway. Ms. Snyder was to be their detention teacher. She was tough but all right, with a funny way of finding humor in any situation. The wrestling coach was heading into the other room with James Lee and friends. And he had no sense of humor at all.

Detention did not pass quickly. Staying after school was bad enough when it was a half hour wasted. When it was all the classes after lunch *and* a half hour after school, detention was torture.

Sammy tried to do his homework, but he was somehow reluctant to work on it. Still, homework was all they let you do in detention. He picked up his pen, opened his notebook, and . . . and started to write a song instead. He had a first line and nothing else. "The sword of boredom hangs over my head . . . "

He looked over at Skink who was deep into a math book. *No help there.* He glanced over at the James Lee crew member imprisoned with them. The boy stared at him through ice-blue eyes, all leather-clad menace.

Shuddering, Sammy looked away.

*Why do they hate me? Why do they hate Skink?* He bit his bottom lip and got a sudden inspiration. *They hate everybody. They probably don't even like themselves.* That made him chuckle. *Of course, what's to like?*

"Something funny, Bug?" the boy hissed, probably hoping that only Sammy would hear. But Ms. Snyder could hear a leaf hit the ground from a tree three blocks away—probably why she was the best of the detention teachers.

"Mr. Addison! No talking! You know the rules." She peered sourly over her glasses at him. "Lord knows you've been in here with me often enough this year, Erik. That seat must be imprinted on your bottom."

Sammy worked hard not to grin and waited for Erik to say something snide back, but instead, he seemed to deflate before Ms. Snyder's criticism and humor.

"Sorry, Ms. Snyder," he said.

*Rather meekly,* Sammy thought.

"I don't know why you get yourself in so much trouble anyway," Ms. Snyder said, though she was no longer looking at Erik. As the teacher, she got to bring a book to detention.

*Lucky her.*

Ms. Snyder turned a page and went on as if reading from a script. "You're such a smart boy." She paused, looked up. "Too smart for this kind of behavior."

Sammy almost choked. *Smart? Erik? He's a no-neck, lizard-brained, ignoram-a-saurus!*

"Yes, Ms. Snyder."

*Yep*, Sammy thought, a bit triumphantly, *that is definitely meek*.

"And until you started hanging around Jamison and his crew—if you can remember that far back—you were a straight A student."

"Just luck, Ms. Snyder."

"Well, luck is what you make it, Erik. Luck and choices." She was again looking at her book, and the conversation seemed to be over.

Erik turned away from Ms. Snyder, from Sammy and Skink, and started staring out the window. His back was rigid. Sammy couldn't tell if it was with embarrassment or anger. Or both.

He didn't want to join one of James Lee's friends in any kind of activity, but after a moment, Sammy stared out the window, too. There was nothing else to do. And he had a lot to think about. About Erik Addison and his A's and what made him choose the Jamison Lee crew.

About bullying and bullies and whether it was worth fighting back.

"Mr. Greenburg!" Ms. Snyder's shout was Sammy's first clue that he'd dozed off.

*Oh, no, I'll probably get* more *detention for that.*

But Ms. Snyder was just alerting him to the fact that the intercom had buzzed and his father was there to pick him up.

"But, why is he . . ." Sammy began, and then he remembered. Hebrew lessons. He wondered idly if it was his grandfather's illness that made his parents decide he needed to be bar mitzvahed. Or if this happened to all almost-thirteen-year-old Jewish boys. One day not religious, the next day . . . in Hebrew class.

He'd totally forgotten today was the day for his first Hebrew lesson, and only now recalled that both the temple and teacher were forty miles away.

*This day's just gone from bad to worse.* Sammy put his chin in his hands.

"Mr. Greenburg," Ms. Snyder said again. "Your father . . ."

Sammy rose slowly, rolled his eyes at Skink, and headed toward the door. The temple was miles away and class started too soon after school for Dad to wait for the bus to bring Sammy home.

But before Sammy got to the door, Ms. Snyder nodded at Skink as well. "You, too, Mr. Williams. You are evidently carpooling with Mr. Greenburg. So you can leave now, too."

"Carpooling . . ." Sammy stuttered, but Skink was quicker on the uptake.

"Yeah, carpooling, doncha, like, remember?" Skink grabbed his books and made for the door. "Guess I'll see you tomorrow, Ms. Snyder."

"Yeah, um, tomorrow," Sammy muttered, and exited after Skink as quickly as he could.

Neither one of them bothered to look back at Erik, who was still staring out the window.

Sammy's dad drummed his thick potter's fingers on the wheel as Sammy and Skink piled into the already-running car.

"Let's go, boys. I don't want us to be late. Your mom says Rabbi Chaim is a stickler for promptness." He checked his watch briefly before returning to his drumming. As soon as seat belts were fastened he gunned the car out of the school lot.

"Thanks for, like, busting us out," Skink said.

Sammy's dad looked at Skink in the rearview mirror, then back at the road. "Sammy and I have to get to Carston before four for his Hebrew lessons. I told your mother I'd pick you up, too, since I was going to be at the school anyway. And your house is kind of on the way." Then he grinned as he signaled a left turn. "And besides, detention is a drag." He turned and gave Sammy as long a look as he dared while driving. "Doesn't mean I'm not disappointed, son. A *week* of detention? What did you do? Steal money from the principal?"

Sammy looked down. "A fight," he said. "Not my fault, though."

"It really wasn't," Skink said. "He was just trying to help me. Now, like, tell me about these Hebrew lessons. My mom and dad speak some Hebrew, from their time in Israel. They use it when they want to say something in front of me they don't want me to understand. I'd love to go with you and learn some. Maybe surprise them when they're spilling secrets!"

"Hey—I've got an idea. Why not let *him* do my bar mitzvah?" Sammy said. "Make everybody happy."

His dad grinned, shook his head. "Nice try, Sammy.

But it doesn't work that way. For starters—Skink isn't even Jewish."

"And for another," Skink said, "I'm already fourteen."

"Nice try, too, Skinner," Sammy's dad said. "I have a sixty-year-old cousin-in-law who just converted to Judaism and had a bar mitzvah. It's really a way of confirming one is now a man and Jewish."

Skink and Sammy slapped palms.

"I'm the man!" Sammy said.

"Not yet," his dad said. "Not *quite* yet." He pulled over and picked up his cell phone. "But I'll call your parents, Skinner, and tell them you're going to spend the afternoon with us in Hebrew school."

Skink's mother picked up on the second ring and actually loved the idea. "But tell him not to get his hopes up. If he learns enough Hebrew to understand us, we'll just switch to Korean."

Mr. Greenburg related the conversation to the boys with a laugh.

"Okay, on to Carston, then," he told them. "This is the Bar Mitzvah Boogie Bus. I think you boys will like Chaim Handleman. He's an Israeli, a music teacher, and—so I'm told—the best bar mitzvah coach this side of Chicago." He turned back onto the street and from there to the interstate.

Along the way to Carston, Sammy and Skink made up a song.

"Maybe the first original the band will do," Sammy said. They called it "Bar Mitzvah Boogie."

"A work in progress," Skink said.

"Not a *lot* of progress," Sammy added.

But in fact, they got the first two verses done. Sammy scribbled them in his English class notebook. Putting them down somehow made the band real.

> *Going down the road*
> *In the bar mitzvah bus,*
> *Boogie and klezmer*
> *And fusion 'R' Us.*
> *Making some music*
> *And making a fuss.*
> *Going down the road*
>
> *(Chorus)*
> *Going down the road,*
> *Going down the road.*

*Rolling and rocking*
*To get there on time,*
*Learning some Hebrew*
*And rhythm and rhyme.*
*Trying some Hebrew*
*And speaking with Chaim.*
*Going down the road.*
*(Chorus)*

"I bet that's the first time the name Chaim was ever in a rock song," said Skinner. "A *klezmer* jazz boogie pop fusion rock song!"

"Maybe," Mr. Greenburg said, banging out the rhythm on the steering wheel as the boys read the words off the page with an ever-increasing driving beat.

"No maybes." Sammy was adamant. "This band has *no maybes* in it." But inside, he knew that it was full of maybes. The first being that maybe Julia Nathanson would join.

And maybe not.

Sammy hadn't thought about it much, but he'd really expected his bar mitzvah teacher to be a wrinkled old rabbinical scholar with a long white beard and eyes squinty from long hours poring over the Torah, the scrolls of the Old Testament. A sort of peaceful walking Bible.

Chaim Handleman was nothing like that. He appeared to be in his midthirties, thin but not gaunt, with dark hair that looked like it had just grown out of an army crew cut. Sammy suddenly remembered that all Israelis served in the army when they turned eighteen, which would explain the haircut but nothing else.

"*Shalom aleichem*," Chaim said to Sammy's dad who answered, "*Aleichem shalom*." Then he turned to Sammy, "And *shalom* to you as well, Samson." He had a soft accent, as if his vowels were produced just a little bit farther back in the throat than other people's.

"Um . . . *shalom*.

Instead of being peaceful, Rabbi Chaim emanated an energy that was making Sammy tired just looking at him. He tapped his feet and nodded his head and stopped waving his arms around just long enough to shake hands.

"Seems there's someone extra here," Chaim said, pointing with one hand at Skink and the other at their surrounds. "Are you Jewish, converting, or just plain curious?" He didn't wait for an answer, but went on talking, now with a hand over his heart as he nodded enthusiastically at Skink. "You're welcome no matter which. What's your name?"

"Skinner John Williams, sir. But please call me Skink. And just, like, plain curious. My parents lived in Israel for a while."

Chaim stopped moving about and put a finger on the side of his nose, as if considering what Skink had just said. His stillness was as complete as his energy had been moments before. Then slowly, Chaim leaned forward and said to both boys, as if they were the two most important people in the world, "Curiosity is the beginning of knowledge. Without curiosity, we are not only lower than the angels, but lower than the animals. Lower than the whale—in Hebrew—*livyatan*. Lower than a dog. In Hebrew *kelev*. Even lower than a slug."

Both Sammy and Skink had mouthed *livyatan* and *kelev* after Chaim, and Sammy added, "What's slug in Hebrew?"

"Good, good, you are curious, too," Chaim said. He was moving about again. Pushing two chairs close together for the two boys, gesturing for them to sit.

Then he signaled with another wave of his arm that Mr. Greenburg should sit farther away.

"You go there, Mr. Greenburg, where the rest of the chairs are gathered together in a kind of minyan."

"Does *minyan* mean slug?" Skink asked.

Rabbi Chaim doubled over in laughter. There was a round skullcap clipped to his sparse hair, blue with gold squiggles on it.

"I know that one," Sammy said. "My grandfather always was part of a minyan, which means part of a group of men who pray a lot."

"Ten men or women actually," Chaim said, now serious again. Then he added: "*Shablul.*"

Sammy worried that maybe his Hebrew teacher was seriously deranged and looked at him strangely.

Chaim caught the look and laughed. "It means slug in Hebrew." His right forefinger moved about, slug-like. Grinning he added, "So you already have three important words in Hebrew. *Livyatan. Kalev. Shablul.*"

"And minyan," Skink said. "Ten Jews."

"Ten people praying," Sammy added.

The rabbi smiled. "But mere words are not enough." He leaned toward the boys.

Without meaning to, the boys leaned in as well.

"First we must learn the alphabet. *Alef. Bet.*"

Skink laughed. "We know the alphabet."

"Not the *Hebrew* alphabet, Master Skink," Chaim walked over to the blackboard, saying over his shoulder, "The Hebrew alphabet is often called the *alefbet*, because of its first two letters."

"But alphabet's an English word," said Skink.

"Borrowed," Chaim told him. "English is a language of brilliant borrowings. I love it. But Hebrew—Hebrew is both a holy tongue and a reborn tongue. It is an ancient language, used in the Torah, the Bible, for study, for the words of G-d. But when the land of Israel was founded, the people needed a newer language, with words for things like truck and tractor and airplane, for things like television and computer and nuclear physics. So Hebrew was reborn." He picked up a large piece of poster board that had been leaning against the wall and brought it back to the boys, before turning it around. "But for you right now, it is important to understand that Hebrew uses a different alphabet than English. So before you can learn Hebrew, you must learn to read the Hebrew alphabet."

Sammy and Skink gawked at the poster board. The letters were simply a bunch of strange symbols that made no sense.

"Also, note that Hebrew goes from right to left, rather than left to right as in English," Chaim added. Again the pointing finger, this time underlining the entire top line.

"Wow!" Skink said. "That's strange."

"Strange? The Russians have Cyrillic letters, the Greek's have Greek letters, Chinese and Japanese have their own letters." Chaim's voice was patient, as if he'd heard this before.

"I meant reading right to left."

"Chinese gets read up and down," Sammy pointed out.

Chaim nodded. "So, *not* so strange after all." He pointed to something that looked vaguely like a fat *N* crowding the right side of the top row. "Here is *aleph* the first letter of the Hebrew alphabet. And this. . . ." the pointing finger went to the last dark splodge to the left of the final line. It looked a bit like an unfinished building or a door. "This is *taw* and is the last letter."

"We have to learn that?" asked Sammy. "*All* that?"

"You *will* learn that," Chaim corrected. "After curiosity comes determination and hard work. Let us begin."

And they did.

They struggled with the alphabet until the heavy black letters were indelible blots in Sammy's brain. He thought he would dream of them any time he fell asleep.

Before they were ready to leave, Chaim gave them each a piece of paper with the entire alphabet on it with the transliterated sound in English written underneath.

"Remember, right to left," he told them. "Practice together. It will be easier that way."

They took the papers. Sammy shoved his into his backpack. Skink folded his carefully three times, creasing each fold till it looked like a pleat on a soldier's trousers.

"And Sammy, your birthday is when?"

Startled by the sudden change in direction, Sammy stuttered. "Uh . . . April tenth."

"Ah, yes, wait." Chaim spun on his heel, went to a bookcase, almost danced in front of it, took down a book bound in red leather, came back. His fingers sprinted through the pages till he came to the one he wanted. "Ah, yes, I thought so." The finger tapped against the page. "Your Torah portion will be about Samson. The mighty hero. He killed many enemies of Israel with a jawbone of an ass, but a woman found out the secret of his strength and . . ."

"I *know* that story," Sammy blurted out.

Chaim became still again. That complete stillness. He looked carefully at Sammy and finally said, "*Do* you? I think you will find out more about it than you think. You will find out what makes a hero . . . and unmakes him."

"*We* could, like, use a hero," mused Skink.

"Meaning?"

"Well," Sammy jumped into the conversation, "there's these bullies at school, and they jumped Skink and stuck my head in the toilet and . . ."

"What!!!!" Sammy's father was up on his feet. "You didn't tell us about the toilet, Sammy. Why didn't you tell us about that?"

Sammy shrugged. "It was no big deal . . ."

Rabbi Chaim made an odd noise deep in his throat and interrupted. "Bullying is *always* a big deal," he said. "For the bullies as well as those they prey upon. That's why Reb Judah Loew, the chief rabbi of Prague, made a golem." He spun away from them, went over to the bookcase, then came back with a small black book that he held up for them to see. It was definitely old, and looked to be made of leather, with gold lettering in a Germanic font.

*Possibly real gold*, Sammy thought, because the letters seemed to glow with some kind of inner light. He read aloud: "'*The Golem*, by Gustav Meyrink.'"

"A golem," Chaim continued, "made of clay, animated by the name of God, to stand as protector of the Jews when death threatened them all."

"A story, boys." Mr. Greenburg said. "As someone who works with clay, I can't begin tell you how hard it is to make something that big."

"The Chinese did, Mr. Greenburg," Skink said. "You know, the terra-cotta army? We've been studying that in art class."

Sammy barely heard them. Not knowing why, he'd reached out for the book, but Chaim pulled it back protectively.

"Sounds like a good story," Sammy said, somewhat breathlessly. The golden letters still glowed.

"It *is* a good story, Samson," Chaim told him. "But like all good stories, the ending will surprise you." He returned the book to its place on the shelf.

Sammy memorized where Chaim put the golem book. A thought had formed in his head the moment the rabbi had first mentioned the golem. No, even earlier— when the letters on the book's cover had begun to glow. No matter how he tried to ignore it, the thought kept popping up: *What if it's true?*

Chaim turned back to them, hands empty once more. "That is enough about the golem. His story is best unsaid and unread. I apologize for bringing it up." He made a funny sound, like a short, sharp laugh of a single syllable. "Hah! And so why, Chaim, did you mention it at all?" he addressed himself. "Because . . ." he answered his own question, "because we were talking about bullies." Glancing at his watch, he added, "In fact, that's enough until our next meeting."

"Which is . . .?" Mr. Greenburg asked.

"Thursday," Chaim said. "Sammy has a lot of work to do if he is to be ready for his bar mitzvah by the spring."

And with that Chaim began whisking them out of

the classroom, out of the temple, shooing them on with waving arms and clucking tongue as if they were a flock of recalcitrant chickens.

*Recalcitrant*, thought Sammy. *A good word.* He started listing synonyms for recalcitrant in his head as if they could keep the other thought—the golem thought—out of it. *Ornery. Uncontrollable. Defiant. Rebellious.*

But it was no use.

*I need that book!* The glowing gold letters called to him. Turning, he ran back to the small classroom.

*I need that book!*

Past the *bimah*, past long benches with their book rests, almost to the door, it was all Sammy could think about.

*I need that book!*

"Left my homework behind!" he exclaimed, stopping at the door. It was even true. His backpack with his homework—both for school and now for Hebrew class as well—was sitting beneath his chair in Chaim's classroom.

Chaim stopped and assumed his finger-on-the-side-of-the-nose stance.

"Well, go grab it," Sammy's father said. "We haven't got all day." He turned to the rabbi, shrugged. "If his head weren't tied to his neck, he'd lose it on a daily basis."

"Boys that age . . ." Chaim began, and both men chuckled.

Almost before his father was done speaking, Sammy was into the classroom. Ignoring his backpack, he ran straight to the bookshelf. He didn't need to search; he knew right where the book was.

*Even if I hadn't seen Chaim put it away, I'm sure I could have found it on my own.*

He touched the book's spine. It felt warm, almost pulsing under his fingers, as if alive.

*I need this book!*

He stuffed the book into his backpack between his science homework and his snack box. He knew if he stopped to think, he'd realize how wrong it was to take the book without asking. *I'm just borrowing it after all.*

The thought of returning the book was even worse than the shame of taking it, and so Sammy decided not to think about it at all, and with that he walked as calmly as he could back to where his father, his friend, and the rabbi waited.

Rabbi Chaim still stood with his finger to his nose, seemingly deep in thought. Sammy didn't dare look him in the eye. Face burning, heart pumping, Sammy knew if he wasn't careful, he would blurt out a confession.

*And then he'd take my book back.*

But Chaim only said, "See you next week, boys."

Sammy mumbled something in return, and then they were safe in the car with Skink in front this time and Sammy in back, squeezing his backpack to his chest like a drowning man with a life preserver.

After a few silent miles, Sammy's father said, "Well, Rabbi Chaim is certainly a character."

"I like him," Skink said.

"Me, too," Sammy's father said. "How about you, Sammy?"

"Hrmm?" Sammy wasn't really paying attention. He'd managed to slip the book out of his backpack and, protected from view by his science folder, had started reading: *And he shall not eat, nor drink, nor accept any pay, but he will protect you from harm and do your work and your bidding.* Sammy thought, *It doesn't sound like a story, it sounds like a manual.*

"Sammy!"

"Erg . . . what? Yeah, Chaim's great." And he went back to reading.

Skink and Sammy's father kept chatting, quickly leaving the subject of Chaim and moving on to pottery and school and how they thought the Bears were doing this season.

Sammy kept reading, but wasn't able to finish the book before they got home. And with Skink staying till just before dinner, he wasn't going to be able to get back to the book any time soon. Besides, his father had other plans for the two of them.

"You've got homework, Samson." And when his father said *Samson* there was never any point arguing. "I'm sure Skink has some, too. Why don't you both go into the basement and work on it together? Your mother will give a shout when his father gets here to take him home. I've got some stuff to do, too. The clay never sleeps." It was something he said often.

Down in the basement, Skink snagged Sammy's just-barely-bigger-than-a-toy keyboard off the music area bookshelf and began plunking away.

"That doesn't look like homework, Skink," Sammy said, channeling his father's voice, though smiling.

Skink smiled back over the keyboard. "I did mine already. In detention." The melody he was playing turned suddenly martial and he boomed out, in a fairly good approximation of the major's tones, "No one gets leave when there's potatoes to be peeled!"

Sighing, Sammy plopped into the folding chair. "I'd rather peel potatoes than do algebra. But I finished in detention, too. I've got a better idea anyway."

Skink raised an eyebrow at him.

"A way to get back at James Lee."

Skink stopped playing and shook his head. "Just ignore them, Sammy." He plinked a few random notes. "They'll move on to softer targets soon."

"That just paints a big bull's-eye on some smaller kid," Sammy said. "But I've got an idea that will take care of the problem permanently, and without us having to raise a finger." He chuckled. "'Cause believe me, I *definitely* don't want to fight them again."

"All right. What's your plan, Word Man?"

"We'll make a golem!"

Skink snorted. "Sure. Like that'll work. Frankenstein lives."

"*I'm* sure." Sammy shot up out of his chair. "We've got all the clay and pottery tools we need in my dad's workshop." He reached the stairs and spun around. Then he marched back toward Skink. "I've thrown a pot or two with my dad, and he's got plenty of pottery books lying around if we get stuck." He reached Skink and stopped. "C'mon . . ."

Skink shook his head and went back to playing the keyboard.

Sammy frowned and pulled the book out of his pack and opened it to a page number he'd memorized.

Skink gasped when he saw the book. "Did you steal that from Rabbi Chaim?"

"Borrowed it," he lied. "Here's the best part—the spell!"

Skink sighed and squinted at the page, scanning down to where Sammy's finger pointed at some dark splodges. "Yeah, except it's in, like, Hebrew!"

Sammy grinned. "And we'll be reading that soon enough. Besides, there's a complete translation in the back." He pointed to the front of the book because, of course, in Hebrew things went back to front, as he'd just learned.

Skink said hesitantly, "You're, like, insane. Maybe that's why we're friends."

"Mad? You call me mad?" Sammy cackled in his best mad-scientist voice. Throwing the golem book aside, he raised clenched fists over his head. "I may be mad, but I'll bring this clay to LIFE!!!"

Shaking his head, Skink turned back to the keyboard and twisted the martial melody he'd been playing earlier into a Klezmer scale. Then he sang:

> *"To life, to life*
> *I'll bring the clay to life.*
> *Frankenstein, he made a monster*
> *and made a monster's wife.*
> *He robbed the local graveyard,*
> *which caused some local . . ."*

"STRIFE!" Sammy shouted.

"Good word, Word Man!"

Sammy grinned at the compliment. "Good Words 'R' Us! Rhymes, too."

Skink nodded. "Yeah, I—like—noticed. And he began to sing again.

> *"He robbed the local graveyard,*
> *which caused some local strife.*
> *Then villagers attacked him with pitchforks . . ."*

He paused. "What else rhymes with life?"

"Knife!" Sammy said smoothly. "With pitchfork, ax, and knife . . ."

"Right!"

> " . . . *with pitchfork, ax, and knife.*
> *But me, I won't be troubled 'cause*
> *I'll bring this clay to life!*"

Sammy hooted with glee and added a doo-wop backing vocal that consisted of, "*Go-lemmmmmmmm. Go-lemmmmmmmm.*"

When Skink heard the backups, he couldn't continue for laughing. Sammy joined in and soon they just alternated between laughing and shouting, "*Go-lemmmmmmmm.*"

Eventually, they ran out of gas, and Sammy said, "But seriously, let's make a golem."

"You're crazy, man."

"C'mon, give me one good reason why not?"

Skink ticked reasons off on his fingers. "It won't work. It's a waste time. It's just a story, Sammy. And it's, like, childish."

"Childish? Are *you* an adult all of a sudden?"

"More than you, I guess."

Sammy wouldn't let it rest. "So even without a bar mitzvah?"

"I just . . ."

Sammy's mom shouted down the stairs, "Skink, your dad's here!"

Whatever Skink had been about to say was lost. Instead, in a gesture of goodwill, he held his fist up and Sammy punched knuckles with him. "See you tomorrow."

"Yeah. Tomorrow, Skink." But Sammy's voice was cool, and Skink had already bounded up the stairs when he added, "I just thought it'd be fun."

He stood looking up at the empty stairs for a few seconds more, than shook himself.

*He'll come around*, he told himself. *Friends help friends.*

He was sure of it because now the Hebrew letters of the spell glowed in his mind. *And I'm going to build that golem. With or without Skink.* Humming the *golem . . . golem* backup line from the song, he settled down in his chair to finish reading the book. The front of the book, which was actually the back, had the English translation.

*There's More to Friendship...*

At the dinner table, Sammy's mother remarked in an offhanded way, "You didn't come up to see Skinner off."

"I was . . . involved," Sammy said.

"Too involved to say good-bye to your friend?" His father was also puzzled.

"He understood."

"He *seemed* a little miffed." Sammy's mother passed him some mashed potatoes.

"*Miffed.* That's a strange word," Sammy said, jumping up from the table to look the word up in the dictionary. "It means annoyed. And it goes back as far as England in the early seventeen hundreds."

"I *know* what it means, Sammy. Finish your dinner."

His father added, "Well, young Skinner only goes

back as far as his house and he's in his early fourteens. But at a guess, he's as miffed as one gets. Really, Sammy, it's not like you have friends dropping off of trees."

"Harry!" his mother cautioned.

Sammy knew that was true, and suddenly he *was* worried. *What if Skink really* was *miffed or annoyed or ticked off? What if his one friend and protector had just become his ex-friend and ex-protector?* He shivered. And then he realized that if the golem project worked, he wouldn't need Skink. Or anyone. Just the Big Ugly Guy. He could almost see the golem already: a hulking, skulking, loyal presence.

Then he thought: *Don't be ridiculous. It won't work. It can't work. It's a fairy tale, a fantasy.*

"He understood," Sammy repeated. "Skink understands." *But does he?*

The spell suddenly glowed, as if in 3-D before him. He almost reached out to touch it with his fingers. At the last minute he stopped himself. He could see it but his parents couldn't. No need to alert them that something strange was going on. But now he knew—with absolute and total conviction—that once his folks were asleep, he would make a golem. He was the perfect person to do it after all. There was all the stuff in his father's workshop.

And his great need for the help a golem had to give.

*But I'll have to go there late at night and in secret.* It was important that no one stop him. *NO* one. Not Skink, not his parents, and certainly not his own somewhat timorous heart.

Sammy set his alarm clock for one a.m. Since his parents slept on the other side of the house, they'd never hear it. Especially since he put it on to play soft music, not the loud, persistent tone. Since he'd fibbed about doing all his algebra, he finished that, then read some more of the translation in the golem book, and fell asleep. It seemed like only a minute or two after he shut his eyes that he heard the sound of WRQC's late night DJ. Rolling over, he slammed his hand on the shutoff button and sat up. Then putting his robe on over his pjs, and wearing his brown fuzzy slippers—looking more like a hobbit on the road to Mordor than someone about to make a monster—he stuffed the golem book in the robe's pocket so no one would find it, and headed out of his bedroom.

He stopped in the hallway, listening. The grandfather clock ticked loudly in the living room, but other than that, the house was still. Nodding to himself, he slunk along the hall until it branched into the living room on the left side, the dining room on the right, then made it quietly, safely to the kitchen.

That was the easy part. The hard part would be opening the kitchen door—it tended to squeak. Or shriek if it was winter. But that was the only way from inside the house to his father's workshop. He pulled slowly on the door, but that only made the squeak last a long, agonizing time.

"Better to do it like a Band-Aid," he told himself. "One quick jerk," and he gave the door a yank. It shrieked once, louder than he'd hoped for—but not so loud as to wake anyone, and then the house was still again.

He propped the door open with his right slipper. No need to make that sound twice.

The workshop was kept at a constant temperature, unlike the rest of the house, which was always cold at night. His father said, "Cold people can always wrap up, but cold clay just gets wrapped up and thrown away."

Sammy went over to the section of the workshop where the clay bricks were kept. He took one from the rear of the pile and then he was back in the kitchen, the door *snicking* quietly closed behind him. He managed to get his foot into his slipper without setting down the clay.

The grandfather clock sang out the half hour in a

clear, ringing voice. Then he heard a toilet flush and he froze. What if his mother or father should come out of their bedroom for a late snack?

Wildly, Sammy looked around for somewhere to stash the clay brick. But before he'd shoved it all the way under the sofa, he heard the sound of the bed sighing as someone lay down.

*Just one of those nighttime toilet trips. Probably Dad.*

Scarcely breathing, Sammy waited for another five minutes, then another, counting the time with the help of the clock, till he heard the sound of his father's snoring. Then clutching the clay to his chest like a new mother with an infant, he tiptoed back to his room.

After closing the door, he turned on the overhead light for just long enough to find the flashlight in his camping bag at the bottom of his closet. Then he turned off the light off, kicked off the slippers, and hopped into bed with the heavy brick of clay, the flashlight, and the golem book still in the pocket of the robe.

Snuggling under the covers, he turned on the flashlight. In the halo of white, he could see to unwrap the clay. It was barely warm from the workshop. He poked a finger into it. Since the clay had not yet been worked, it would take a while for him to make pieces soft enough to start making anything with it. He knew all about that part. His dad had shown him how to do that when he was a kindergartner. He knew all about coiling and making slabs, about shaping figures. However, he was an absolute flop on the wheel; his pieces wobbled and warped. *But*, he thought, *you can't make a golem on a wheel anyway.*

He didn't allow himself to acknowledge that it wasn't actually possible to create a living, breathing golem at all.

He fell asleep before he'd gotten more than a few pieces wedged and worked, and woke covered in bits of clay, sunlight streaming in through his window, his mother knocking on the door.

"Don't make me come in there, mister," she called.

"I'm up, I'm up!" His heart was beating wildly. He leaped out of bed, holding on to the larger part of the clay, and little bits fell onto the floor. Scrambling on his hands and knees he picked up everything he could find and stuck them on the larger piece which he stashed at the bottom of his closet under his sleeping bag. Then he got dressed and was about to leave the room when he thought he'd better check the bed.

*Just in case!*

Lucky he did, because there were about fifteen pieces

of clay the size of the tip of his pinkie sprinkled between the sheets, and a couple even under his pillow.

He added those pieces to the stashed clay, then checked the front of his shirt, saw clay on it, took it off, and shook it out over his trash basket. Then he put his shirt on again, and a sweater over it.

*Just in case.*

Before going to the door, he checked himself in the mirror. "Don't want any clay pox," he whispered to his image, but he looked clean.

Finally, he walked out of the door and into the kitchen as if it were an ordinary day.

*One ordinary day*, he thought, *with a monster.* Even though he hadn't quite gotten started on the golem, he already felt better about going to school.

Sammy's good feeling lasted for about eighteen seconds after he got to school.

Skink wasn't there.

In the week they'd known one another, Skink had always been at school *before* Sammy. Always met him at his locker so they could talk about things, like the Boyz or the band.

Sammy stomped down the hall. *First Julia, now*

*Skink.* He wondered if something was catching—and why *he* couldn't have caught it. Whatever *it* was.

Throwing open his locker, he tossed in his bag and slammed the door shut with a loud clang. *Some friend— leaving me alone to fend off James Lee and his gang.*

Sammy stopped cold. As the enormity of that fact began to sink in, he decided to stop stomping and start skulking. *Just . . . in . . case . . .*

Slipping into homeroom, he went swiftly to the relative safety of his desk. He saw no sign of any of the James Lee's crew.

*Good. Maybe they're late. Or even better, got run over by the school bus.*

He almost began to relax.

But suddenly the door was thrown open, slamming against the wall with a loud bang, louder even than a drummer with a full kit, and in came three of them jostling each other, snickering, bumping fists.

*They look awfully pleased with themselves. Except for Erik Addison. He looks like he swallowed a bug. A BIG bug.*

Erik's buddies grinned at Sammy in a way that made him shiver.

*Whereas those two look like cats that ate a couple of canaries. BIG canaries.*

Even using an extraordinary word like *whereas* didn't give Sammy his usual lift as the three Boyz made their way to the back of the room.

Hunching his shoulders he shivered.

*I hope Skink gets to school soon.*

Sammy got the call before fourth period, just after lunch.

"Sam Greenburg to the office, please. Sam Greenburg to the office."

He'd no idea what he'd done to deserve a trip to Sinner's Row, but backpack over one shoulder, he headed toward the principal's office. It didn't pay to keep the Big Cheese waiting.

But instead of Principal Kraft, Sammy saw his parents outside the school office.

"What's up, folks?" he asked as he walked up.

His mom wiped her eyes quickly and smiled at Sammy.

"Mom? Are you crying?"

"Honey, we came as soon as we heard," she said. "We know how close you are to Skink."

"What happened to Skink?"

Sammy's father answered. "He was beaten up. Badly. We're going to take you to see him in the hospital right away."

The floor tilted strangely, and Sammy had to drop his backpack and put his hand on the wall to keep from falling over. *Skink? Beaten up? Badly? Bad enough for the hospital?*

"Who?" he finally managed.

His father looked at him strangely. "No one knows. We'll take the car, son."

Sammy shook his head. "No. I mean . . . How did Skink?" The floor straightened for him and he scooped his backpack up off the floor. "Let's go."

They ran to the car, and the car's tires squealed as they peeled out of the school parking lot.

Skink was sitting up in bed. He waved at Sammy when he pushed past the major and Mrs. Williams. Sammy tried to smile at Skink, but couldn't. He was too busy checking Skink's condition.

Skink looked bad, both eyes bruised, the left one nearly swollen shut. But he wasn't plugged into any hospital machines and no doctors or nurses hovered around him. Only his parents. Sammy thought those were good signs.

"Hey, Word Man," Skink said. He didn't open his mouth very wide when he spoke, and he didn't smile.

*Probably hurts too much,* Sammy thought. He pointed at Skink's hands which were resting on top of the covers.

Skink understood immediately. "The hands are okay. Actually, everything's pretty okay. Considering."

"Considering . . ." murmured Mrs. Williams from behind Sammy.

"I don't know, Skink" Sammy said, pointing at Skink's black eyes. Even against his dark skin the bruises were noticeable. "You *are* in the hospital."

Skink shrugged. And winced slightly. "They just want to hold me overnight and make sure I don't have, like, a concussion."

"You get knocked out?"

"Nope. I remember the whole thing."

"Then what happened, Skink?"

"Yes, what happened, Skinner?" a new voice asked.

Sammy hadn't noticed that there was another person in the room. But when he turned to find the voice, he saw a policeman sitting in a chair by the window, fully uniformed except for his hat, which lay on the sill behind him.

"I told you," Skink answered the policeman, chuckling without much humor, "I got my butt kicked." He looked at Sammy. "It would have been worse but some neighbors heard the noise and chased them off before they could, like, really put the boots to me."

The policeman had a notebook in his hand, but it didn't look like Skink was giving him much to write in it.

"And you didn't see who did it?" the policeman said in a tired, controlled voice. *As if,* Sammy thought, *he'd asked it before.*

"They wore masks. I don't think you want me to pick the Power Rangers out of a lineup."

The policeman looked like he was about to stand up, then changed his mind. "Well, let's go through it again. Besides the masks, what were they wearing?"

Skink frowned. "I'm sorry, officer. I really can't help you. I was too busy staying alive to notice anything else."

"Did they say anything?" the policeman asked. "I mean, racial things?"

*Hate crime?* For a moment Sammy's heart lifted. *If the police could get the Boyz on a hate crime charge . . .* Then he realized that just hating an outsider, a newcomer didn't count.

"Nope," Skink said. "Nothing particularly racial. In fact they didn't say anything at all. All they did was breathe loudly. Turns out beating someone up is, like, hard work."

There was something going on here that Sammy
didn't understand. *Why doesn't he tell them about James
Lee and his Boyz? It* had *to be them.* He was about to open
his own mouth when the major spoke.

"Skinner John. Son. Who. Did. This." He clipped
off each word as if he were biting off strips of beef jerky.
Sammy looked up at him and realized that if there were
a definition in the dictionary for "barely contained
fury," next to it would be a picture of Major Williams
in this hospital room. His teeth were clenched so hard
Sammy was surprised he'd been able to force air past
them to speak even the six words he had. His fists were
so tight, his fingers were nearly white. His eyes showed
no human emotion Sammy could name.

"I don't know who did it, sir." Skink didn't look at
the major. "I think I need to rest. Mom? Can you get
the nurse?"

Sammy waited for the major to say something
about "nurse to hearse," but his jaw was clenched tight,
with only a slight whistling of air escaping through his
teeth.

"Oh!" Mrs. Williams said. "Of course, I'm sorry,
honey." She gave a half bow to the policeman. "Can we
do this later?"

"Of course, ma'am." He grabbed his hat, nodded to the major, and ducked out. Sammy started to follow.

"Sammy, wait a sec," Skink said. "I need to know what Mr. Hallas gave us for homework today."

Sammy stopped while Mrs. Williams, her slim arm tightly wound about the major's strained biceps, dragged him out. Sammy's parents followed close at their heels.

When they were all gone, Sammy took the cop's chair. "Who's Mr. Hallas?"

Skink shrugged again, then, with nobody but Sammy left in the room to see, grimaced in pain. "My humanities teacher. And I know you're not in that class. But I had to talk to you alone."

"It was James Lee wasn't it?"

"They *did* wear masks." He sat up a bit taller. "But it had to be."

"We've got to tell the cops! And your dad!"

Skink shook his head. "The cops can't do anything. They wore masks. And you—like—can't say anything to my dad!"

Sammy thought of the major's clenched fists, his dead eyes. "He'll kill them, won't he?"

"He'll at least hurt 'em, like, bad. And I don't want to be responsible for him going to prison."

"We've got to do *something*!"

Skink gave a very small smile. "Well, what I'm going to do is, like, heal. And then train."

"Train?"

"Yeah, apparently I need more practice in fighting multiple opponents." Skink chuckled at his own joke, though it sounded forced, and probably hurt him some to laugh.

Sammy joined in even though the joke wasn't actually funny. Skink looked like he needed someone to laugh with. And *that* was what friends were for.

In the car home, Sammy's dad said nothing, but his mom turned around, as much as the seat belt allowed.

"It was that awful gang in school, wasn't it? The ones who pick on you, Sammy."

"I asked him that, Mom. But he said they were masked, so he couldn't be sure."

His dad almost growled. It was a sound low in his throat. A sound Sammy had never heard him make before.

"But he doesn't want his dad to get in trouble, so don't even hint at that." Sammy spoke with as much authority as he could manage. "I mean, what if it was someone else."

His dad banged a palm on the steering wheel. "My Lord, Sarah, we haven't come very far in race relations in this country if a gang of kids can beat up someone just because he's black."

"Half black, dear. He's also half Korean."

"That's not why they beat him up." Sammy's voice was low, but sure.

His dad's hands on the wheel were so tight, they seemed glued there.

Sammy continued. "They beat him up because they're scared of him. He knows martial arts. He's fast and efficient and not scared." He paused. "Not like me."

"Well, I'm going to the principal and tell him what I suspect," his mother said.

"MOM!" Sammy shouted in panic. "You can't . . ."

His mom sighed. "If you're *that* scared, Sammy, why not let me homeschool you this year. I can do it. I used to be a teacher. Well, a teacher's assistant. If we can't even *report* bullying for fear of reprisals . . ."

"It's not reprisals that I'm afraid of, Mom . . ." he

began, then stopped, wondering how much he'd give away if he said more.

His dad glanced sideways at his mom. "Honey, have you *looked* at Major Williams? He'll kill those kids with one hand if he suspects them at all, and never give it a second thought. He's a trained military man, a . . ."

Sammy barely heard them. He was thinking about homeschooling. It was tempting. Really tempting. But then he thought about Julia Nathanson. He thought about Skink. He thought about . . . the golem.

"I got it covered," he told them both, without telling them anything.

Dad's hands relaxed on the wheel. "That's my boy," he said. But it didn't sound to Sammy like he really meant it.

Sammy didn't go back to school that day, and was actually relieved, though he didn't let his parents know. Three times he overheard his mother talking on the phone about what had happened. Twice he was sure it was to Skink's mom, and once—maybe—to an authority, but whether the authority was the policeman or the principal or the major he wasn't sure, because just then she spotted Sammy, put her hand over her mouth, and walked with the phone into the workshop where she closed the door behind her.

Sammy took a deep breath. *What does it matter who she's talking to?* he told himself. He had the afternoon to himself. Not being in school, he would be able to reread the golem book cover to cover again—well, at least the English translation part—and memorize the important parts of it. Only this time, he'd see if he could figure out how the golem could protect not one but two people.

*Skink and me.*

That night, as Sammy lay in bed, he ran through his possible choices. Though he'd told his parents he had everything covered, it was a lie. Without Skink, he didn't stand a chance. But if he stayed home, he'd never see Skink again. He'd never see Julia Nathanson. Never have a band. Or a life.

He put his right hand to his head and swore he could hear the wheels grinding away in there. He thought: *The golem is a fairy tale. Not real. Not possible. And yet . . .*

Sammy sat up in bed, but quietly. Maybe he should check the clay anyway. Just . . . well, just in case.

But then he heard a noise. Listened intently for a moment. Realized it was his parents talking in the living room. They didn't sound happy. He lay back down. This was not the moment.

He looked up at the ceiling, a dark splodge in the dark room. And then, suddenly everything became as clear as if a lightbulb had suddenly been turned on. Fairy tale or not, Sammy knew what he had to do. He had to work on the golem again. *Really* work this time. Work—and believe. It was his last—in fact it was his *only*—chance.

Turning onto his side, he reached for his clock-radio and set the alarm to one a.m. again. Then he snuggled down into the covers and slept. He dreamed of James Lee chasing him through a jagged landscape. Behind James Lee was a large dark shadow. The background music was klezmer.

He awoke to the sound of soft music, but without thinking, hit the snooze button.

Twice.

"Rats," he hissed, sitting up in the dark. "Twenty minutes already wasted."

There was little enough time. "I need a protector before Skink comes back to school. And I'm the only one who can provide it," he whispered to the room.

He got out of bed carefully, noiselessly. Crossing the room, he gave silent thanks to the cushiony rug. When he opened the closet door, he did it in such tiny increments, there were no awful squeaks. He turned on the closet light knowing that no one could see it from the hallway.

Staring at the few pieces of clay he'd already worked and the remains of the brick, he couldn't help sighing aloud.

*And what kind of protector will I be building out of one brick of clay? Sure, it's twenty-five pounds. But what's that going to get us?* He made a face. *A protector the size and weight of a three-year-old?* He didn't think a two-foot-tall golem was going to help anyone.

"I need more clay!" he whispered, but in the room's silence it sounded like a shout.

*I'll need at least a two-hundred-pound golem, sort of the size and shape of Uncle Manny,* he told himself. In a family of runts, Uncle Manny was a giant. *Of course, he'd married in!* Sammy held his arms out, trying to remember how huge Uncle Manny was.

*I'll need six bricks at least. Plus one for any clay that gets wasted in the process of shaping and another for shrinkage. That's eight. I've got one here. So seven more trips to the garage to haul out nearly two hundred pounds of clay.*

It already sounded like a tough job before he had his next thought: *Seven more trips through the squeaky kitchen door.*

He couldn't do that in one night. One squeak his parents might sleep through. But seven? Not a chance.

Picking up the closeted brick, he hauled it to the bed to begin working . . .

. . . and that's when he realized he'd need to get a full eight bricks. In his hurry to hide the clay away yesterday, he hadn't covered it well enough with the plastic wrapping and it was now too dry to be of any use.

"Stupid, stupid, stupid!" he muttered.

Suddenly, everything about the golem, like the clay, seemed too hard. Not to mention insane.

*Dad might not miss one brick of clay, or even two—but nine?*

Sammy collapsed back onto his bed, suddenly close to tears. The light from the closet threw strange shadows onto the ceiling, as if a dark forest of trees were looking down on him. "It's not just hard—it's impossible."

He began to think the way he did when studying for a math test.

*This is my life test*, he thought. *I can't tell Mom and Dad. They'll think it's crazy. That I'm crazy. And I can't tell the major because it will set him off again. And Skink wouldn't want that. And I can't even tell Skink. But what do I do next?*

The trees in the ceiling didn't provide any answers, so Sammy shifted his gaze back to the ruined block of clay. It looked particularly hopeless from this angle.

*A good Jew would go to his rabbi for advice. But since I stole from mine, that leaves him out, too.*

He lay still for a long moment, gathering his courage, wondering where courage was stored and how a person was supposed to gather it. *With a teaspoon? A shovel? A bucket loader?* His mind was awhirl with such questions. Stupid questions but important questions, too.

*Get up, Sammy,* he told himself. *So what if you don't have many options? You've got this one, and who knows—it just might work.* He shook himself mentally. "It's *got* to work."

He sat up. "Though my closet might get a bit messed up in the process." He laughed at that. His closet was *always* a mess. What did a little more matter?

Sammy thought for another minute. *If I can take two bricks a night from Dad's studio, build the golem from the ground up in my closet—I'll hide him behind my clothes. Then I can fire him on the fifth or sixth night.*

He didn't want to think about firing the clay. Not yet. His father would surely realize something was happening then. *One: the kiln makes a lot of noise. Two: it gets really hot and takes a day to cool down. Three: . . .* Well, there wasn't really a three.

But he did know one thing. One important thing: *Working that way gets me a complete golem in under a week.*

He bit his lip. *I can be invisible for a week. Play nice with James Lee for a week. Give him my homework and my gum for a week. And my allowance. Write him a B paper or an A paper. Though that might be pushing it. No one would believe he could write an A paper.*

He stood up. Slipped into his robe.

*That's if I make it past the squeaky door, again.*

*And again.*

*And again . . .*

He made himself a mental note to find some 3-IN-ONE oil in the morning. Or if necessary some of his mom's cooking oil. Oiling the door should solve the squeaking problem.

*It's all doable one problem at a time.*

Once again in his father's studio, Sammy went to the very back of the stacked clay bricks and found a small pile of four. He figured his father would never miss those.

Taking one back into his room, he spent the next two hours shaping the golem's feet.

He smoothed the clay down with his hands and a putty knife he'd filched from the workshop for some long-ago project and forgotten to return. Then he used the edge of the knife to carve in details like toenails, then pinched ligaments and veins to the surface. The golem's feet ended up a size larger than his own. As his mom liked to say, "You're a small boy for such big feet." Then she would laugh, and add, "The first time I ever got you shoes, the salesman said 'Never mind the shoes, I'll wrap up the boxes they came in.'"

Now his big feet proved perfect as a measure for making the golem. But only the feet. The rest would have to be done by guesswork. The golem had to be much larger than Sammy if it was to work reliably as his protector.

It had to be at least as tall as James Lee, and—he hoped—taller.

Strangely, Sammy was energized by the clay feet . . . and laughed at the joke of them. "My golem protector," he whispered to himself, "has feet of clay!"

He began to giggle. Then he stood, wrapped the feet well in the plastic the clay had come in, and stuck them in the closet.

At that same moment, the start of a new song for the band came to him.

> *I wanted a monster, to feed and to play.*
> *I made him by nighttime, and never by day.*
> *But then I discovered his feet were of clay,*
> *Singing hey and a ho and a go-lem-oh!*

It was awful. *Boy*, he thought, *I must be really goofy from lack of sleep.* But it didn't stop him from going back for a second clay brick.

He woke to a knock on his bedroom door. Sunlight was flooding through

"Sammy . . . you're going to be late," his mother said. "Breakfast is on the table."

"Be right there." He'd fallen asleep before working the second brick, and it was still in its protective plastic wrapping. He got up and hid it in the back of his closet beside the clay feet, then got dressed. At the last minute, he stripped his bed because it was filled with clay bits, and threw the sheets and pillowcases down the laundry shoot they called the "Rabbit Hole."

Opening the door, he called to his mother, "I'm not feeling all that well. And I'm so tired. Maybe I have mono. My sheets were soaked, so I threw them down the Rabbit Hole."

She came in and put a hand to his head. "You do feel a little warm," she said. "I'll let you stay home today, but you'll have to remain in bed."

"No problem," he said, thinking that once he'd slept, he could tell her he was doing a super-secret project for school. *A science project!* After all, didn't the science fiction writer Arthur Clarke say something like "Any sufficiently advanced science is indistinguishable from magic." Or was that technology? Either way, he could talk himself out of anything with his mom.

His dad—that was going to be a harder proposition. *Especially if he finds out there's some missing clay.*

Sammy went into the kitchen to get some breakfast. His dad was already in the studio.

"Eat a little something," his mother said. "I'll get you fresh sheets. Then it's back to bed for you."

He didn't argue. He actually did feel awful. Awful as in tired and scared. Not awful as in sick.

Working on the golem during the day was difficult. His mother kept coming in to check on him. Sometimes she knocked, sometimes she didn't, in case she might be waking him. She was unpredictable. But she always left at least a half hour between visits, so he used that brief window to begin making the golem's legs. He'd no time to pull everything out of the closet, so, kneeling down, he shoved everything but his backside in and began putting clay on top of the feet for ankles.

Measuring with a piece of string he'd found in his desk drawer, he decided the lower part of the golem's legs had to be at least double his own. Quickly forming a rough shape, he then scraped away clay till there was a hint of a shinbone. He took the leavings and packed them onto the back of the calf to form a solid muscle mass, like the picture of the Celtics basketball players he had on a poster over his bed.

Getting ready to carve some detail into the calf muscle, he was startled when his mother knocked.

"Sammy? You awake?"

Sammy hopped back into bed and shoved his dirty hands underneath the sheets.

*I'm going to need to change the bed* again *today.*

"Yeah, Mom."

She came in carrying the thing Sammy had dreaded since he decided to fake an illness: a thermometer. It was a cheap electronic one, probably cost six bucks at Walgreens. And it was going to spell the end of Sammy's charade.

"Let's take your temperature," she said, and popped it in his mouth before he could protest.

He couldn't do anything but think hot thoughts. Couldn't even surreptitiously warm the thermometer in his hands because he'd get clay all over it.

The thermometer beeped and his mother pulled it out, looked closely, and frowned at the result.

"It's normal, Sammy." She gave it a little shake like an old-fashioned mercury thermometer, as if that would change the result. "Ninety-eight-point-six. Couldn't be any more normal if you tried."

Sammy shrugged. Kept his mouth shut.

"You *sure* you're not feeling well?"

"Not really." It was the least he could say.

Sammy's mother sighed and sat down on the edge of the bed, thermometer in her left hand. Her right she placed on his cheek. She looked directly into his eyes.

"Sammy, dear. I'm not a fool. And you don't have to lie to me. Is this about Skink?"

Sammy shook his head. "No, it's—" He stopped as his mother frowned and took her hand away. "Okay, yes. It is. But I *do* want to go back to school. I just need a few days to figure things out."

His mother's expression didn't change. "I won't send you back there to get hurt."

"Mom, I know we can't afford private school. Not that there's any around here, anyway. And moving isn't an option." Even to himself he sounded like an old man. A *scared* old man.

"Homeschool." But she didn't look him in the eyes when she said it.

"Really, Mom?" Sammy watched the breath go out of her. "I don't think you want to devote the next five

years of your life to *my* education." He was about to
reach out of the covers to touch her hand in comfort,
but remembered the clay just time. "I'll be okay."

"How can we know that?" She squeezed the
thermometer till Sammy thought it might break.

"Because I'm no threat to them. Oh, they'll tease
me, but they've done that all along. Skink scared them,
so they had to do something big."

"How big?"

"He showed them he knew martial arts and got the
younger kids laughing at them."

"Ah." Sammy's mom nodded silently, her eyes
starting to shine. "You're very brave, honey."

*I doubt that very much.*

Leaning over, Sammy's mother suddenly enveloped
him in a giant embrace. Sammy hugged her back through
the comforter.

"Just give me a couple of days to get my head
together," he said, "then I'll go back to school." He felt
her nod against his shoulder.

"All right," she said, the words muffled by shoulder
and pillow. She sat up and rubbed at her eyes. "All right,"
she said again. "At least this way I won't have to keep
coming to check up on you."

"That'll help both of us."

She took it to mean Sammy and herself. Or maybe Sammy and Skink.

*He* meant it would help him—and the golem.

Standing, his mother ran her hands down her front as if dusting herself off. "Well, I'll call the school and tell them you're sick so we can get your homework for the next few days."

"Joy."

That brought a weak smile and she stepped to his door. As she left, she said, "I smell clay. Your father must be working up a storm." Then she smiled a little bigger and left, closing Sammy's door behind her.

That first day it was all about the golem's legs. Only the knees gave Sammy a bit of trouble—he hoped the golem would walk all right on the knobby things it ended up with.

The thighs were easy, if possibly a bit large. Well, actually, *way* too large at first. They looked like giant hot dogs. He spent most of his time cutting them down, before building them up again. And shaping them. He'd tried looking at his own legs in the mirror. Very quickly he realized they were no help, being short and skinny and frankly underdeveloped.

The men on the poster had legs like tree trunks. Slim tree trunks.

"I'm not making a basketball player," Sammy reminded himself. "More like a boxer. Or a wrestler." He hauled his computer out of his backpack and googled wrestlers, settling on the young Arnold Schwarzenegger's legs.

When it came to shaping the spot where the legs joined, Sammy copped out and added on a clay pair of shorts. After all, the golem was not going to eat or drink, so why did he need . . . he didn't let his mind wander any further than that.

He was actually relieved when his mother knocked on the door to deliver his homework.

The next day, the midsection went quickly. Sammy had gotten not one but two bricks, after oiling the kitchen door when his parents had gone off grocery shopping together.

He scraped out a set of abs a prizewinning boxer would have been jealous of. Then he made a chest that was both broad and muscled but strangely nippleless. He just couldn't face any more embarrassment.

The rest of the day, he catnapped and did some of his

homework and twice spoke to Skink, who was already home from the hospital.

"My body," Skink said the second time, "is healing, like, inhumanly fast. Or so the doctor says. And I can go back to school in like two days."

"Joy!" Sammy said, and then had to explain that he had stayed out of school until Skink was going back. He didn't mention the golem.

But, Sammy knew any further work on the creature would have to be done at night, and he couldn't very well work the entire night through again. Luckily, Sammy's parents decided to go to see an X-Men movie, both of them surprised when he refused to accompany them.

"I've got a big school project due Monday."

"I don't remember getting any big project assignment for you," his mother said.

Thinking quickly, Sammy said, "It's a long term thing. Just getting a head start." Then he had a brilliant idea. "I'm going to need some clay for it."

His father grinned. "Sure. How much do you need?"

"Maybe three bricks?"

"What are you making—a colossus?"

"Something like that," he said, determined to look up the word as soon as they were gone.

Suddenly things had become dead easy. Sammy was relieved and—somehow—upset. Sneaking was one thing. All teenagers did a bit of that. But straight-out lying to his parents felt awful. Necessary—but awful.

However, as soon as they were gone, and after he looked up colossus—*any statue of gigantic size; huge and powerful*—he got back to work, no longer worrying about sneaking or lying or anything else but the golem. The colossus. The clay man of the hour.

While they were gone, the phone rang three times. Sammy let the machine pick up the first two times but then, on the third time, he happened to be going back for another brick of clay and automatically picked up the phone.

"Greenburg's residence, Sammy speaking," he said. It was something he'd been taught early on since this was his father's business phone as well as the house phone.

"Samson, it's Reb Chaim."

He nearly hung up. As it was, he dropped the phone with one hand and caught it—barely—with the other.

"Um, hello, Rabbi," he said. "I've . . . I've been home sick this week."

"Yes, your mother called to tell me. But it's something else I want to talk about."

*He knows . . .* Sammy thought. *He knows . . .*

"Is there something you want to tell me, Samson?"

He almost wanted to confess everything. Then thinking about the three-quarters of a golem in his closet, he thought better of anything like a confession. It was way too late for that. "Tell you *what*, Rabbi?"

*I am so going to hell*, Sammy thought, for lying to a rabbi. *Even though Jews don't actually believe in hell. At least I don't think we do.*

"I meant about whether you were going to be able to study, while being so sick. And how your friend Skink is doing. Your mother told me about that, too."

"Anything else, Rabbi?"

"Hmmmmm." It was a sound like the noise a plague of locusts might make. "Study hard. I will see you when you get better."

It felt more like a threat than a promise. Sammy hung up carefully. He checked the caller IDs for the two missed calls. Both of them were business stuff. Not the rabbi. He didn't know what to make of the rabbi's questions.

*Are they really so innocent? Or is he just feeling out the situation.* Sammy shook his head. He had no way of knowing without asking. And *asking* was the last thing he could do.

Instead, he went into the studio to get the last brick of clay for the evening, feeling—for the first time—that he really was beginning to get sick. His stomach gurgled and his heart . . . he could feel it beating so fast, it would have made the perfect drum for the band.

Back in the closet once again, he set to work on the golem. Its arms turned out to be a technical challenge. Everything to this point had been built up. Only the arms hung down. Sammy worried about gravity and so he brought his desk chair and a stool into the closet to let the arms rest on until they dried. That helped him while he worked on the elbows.

"Though why God thought elbows necessary . . ." he said aloud. After all, James Lee couldn't elbow him in the gut if he didn't have any. *Elbows, that is, not guts.* "Well, actually, I *don't* have any guts," he told himself, "or I'd stick up for myself." Though somehow he could—occasionally—stick up for someone else.

"Ergo, the golem!" He loved the word *ergo*, meaning something like behold! Or therefore! Or look at this!

Sammy made sure the wet clay was good and sticky as he worked, and afterward—with the help of the chair—there was no gravitationally induced stretching or dismemberments or things that were dropping off the golem, all in all a good thing.

In the middle of the day, when his father was in the studio working on a big order for an upscale catalog company, and his mother was out in the garden weeding the vegetables, he made a copy of the English part of the rabbi's book on their office's small copying machine. He was ready in case his parents asked him what it was he was doing. A school assignment, of course. But no one saw him and so no one asked.

The *colossus* kept growing. Monday it was time for Sammy to make the head.

But first, it was time to drive to Carston for another Hebrew lesson, which might be a bit scary, if the rabbi asked him anything about the missing book. But maybe, Sammy thought, he could get more pointers about the golem as long as he was careful. Learn some important Hebrew words in case the golem only spoke Hebrew. *Whale, dog, slug, alefbet* were not going to cut it.

*And* if pushed, he could always return the book now that he had the important parts copied.

It was a quiet ride to the temple without Skink in the car. Sammy's dad drummed his fingers on the wheel most of the way.

Suddenly Sammy began to worry about the golem book. Was that really why Rabbi Chaim had called? Or might the rabbi—maybe—applaud Sammy's inventiveness. He had the book in his backpack just in case.

Sammy looked out the window and fretted, watching cornfields zipping by, seeing the occasional farmstead breaking the green blur with a flash of white house and outbuildings.

Sammy thought about the clay colossus stuffed in the back of his closet, wondering if he could really turn it into a walking protector, a bully against bullying. It had been an interesting project, sure. But real? He shook his head. *This is the US of A, not Neverland, idiot!*

"*Shalom aleichem*, Samson," Rabbi Chaim said as Sammy and his dad came in.

"*Aleichem shalom*, Rabbi Chaim," Sammy replied.

"Reb Chaim will do. Think of it as a kind of rabbinical nickname," Chaim said with a wink.

Sammy's dad nodded absently.

"Mr. Greenburg," Reb Chaim said, "why don't you

leave Samson and me on our own today. We have a lot to talk about. And if you'll pardon the cliché, there's a coffee shop at the end of the block . . ." He waved vaguely in that direction. ". . . and it has some lovely bagels. I don't know whether they always carried them, or only started when the temple went up, but they're almost as good as a New York deli. Go get yourself one and a cup of coffee, if you partake. Come back in an hour." He looked at his watch. "Five fifteen to be precise."

His dad nodded again. *Like one of those bobblehead dolls*, Sammy thought. He wasn't used to his dad being so compliant, but figured he was just thinking about a design in clay. Then his dad left, giving Sammy a pat on the back before going out the door, leaving Sammy alone with the rabbi.

Once again, Sammy was struck by Chaim's ceaseless energy. The thin man paced as he spoke, his hands, arms—even his eyebrows danced with every word.

Still pacing, Reb Chaim motioned for Sammy to take a chair. Sammy almost missed it in the flurry of Chaim's other random motions. Then Chaim took a chair himself, tapping his foot till Sammy sat. Then he was suddenly still as stone, one finger placed by the side of his nose.

"Looks as if your father has a lot on his mind, Samson." He raised one eyebrow at Sammy. "I imagine you do, as well?"

*He knows!* Sammy tried to show nothing on his face, but he guessed it was turning bright red. Forcing himself to nod, he said, "Tough week at school."

Chaim stared at Sammy for ten tics and then stood and began pacing again.

"Samson," he said, "when young men come to me, it is not my job to teach them Hebrew, or their Torah portion, or perform any of the duties required at their bar mitzvah."

Sammy frowned. "But—"

Reb Chaim shook his head, and went on. "I do all of those things, of course, but that is not my *real* job. They are just the means to an end. And they are not why your father, or any father, leaves his son in my care, or in the care of any rabbi, not for thousands of years."

"Rabbi . . . er, Reb Chaim," Sammy said, "I have no idea what you're talking about." But he did. *He's talking about the book, and he's going to kick me out of Hebrew class. Then he'll call the police and I'll go to jail and my father will disown me and . . . and then they'll find the mess in my closet and I'll be committed and . . .*

Reb Chaim laughed and sat back down. "Of course not, Samson. They teach us to be opaque in rabbi school."

Despite his near panic, Sammy thought, *A new word!* and leaned forward. "What's opaque?"

"Opaque can mean something that is not transparent, but more often it means someone who is hard to understand or who speaks in riddles or stories that have more than one meaning. Because it is important that people think about the stories or riddles, and wrestle with their meanings."

"Could you spell it?"

Reb Chaim laughed. "A word guy! I *knew* I liked you. It's O-P-A-Q-U-E."

Sammy repeated the word and the spelling. It wasn't just that he was a word guy, though. If the rabbi was being opaque, Sammy knew he was being diverting. Keeping the rabbi off dangerous ground. And it seemed to be working.

And the more Reb Chaim talked, the more Sammy calmed down. *Maybe he* doesn't *know. Maybe I'm simply obsessing. Maybe I'm in the clear. And besides, I've just learned a new word.*

"So, Samson," Reb Chaim said, leaning forward and

slapping the desk in front of him lightly. "Why are you here?"

"To learn Hebrew?" Sammy asked.

"Is that an answer or a question?"

"Maybe both?" He wondered if he, not the rabbi, was being opaque.

Reb Chaim shook his head. "I already told you that's *not* why you've come to me."

Frowning, Sammy said, "Then I suppose it's not to learn my Torah portion either."

Reb Chaim grinned. "What is your bar mitzvah for? What happens on that day?"

"It's the day I become a man."

"Do you honestly believe you will become a man on that day?"

Samson hadn't thought about that before. "Um . . . yes?"

Reb Chaim said nothing for a moment, just raised an eyebrow at Sammy and tapped the side of his nose idly. "If that actually happened, Samson, you would be the first boy ever to do so." He placed both his hands palms down on his desk and stared hard into Sammy's eyes. "There is no mystical moment, no instant in time that you can point to and say, 'There! That is when I became a man.' We pick a time because we must. It helps us make a transition. But it's a transition, not an immediate change. And my job—my real job—is to help you start to make that transition from boy to man."

Sammy was almost sure that if Reb Chaim had noticed that the book was gone he would have mentioned it by now. His breathing slowed and it felt like his face was a normal color now. "And how do you do that?"

Reb Chaim laughed and was back on his feet and moving again. "By doing what we Jews do best." He grinned at Sammy. "Talking. So, what's on your mind, Samson? What's got your father so preoccupied? And what do you need to know to become a man in your family?"

*He doesn't even* suspect *the book is gone.* Sammy sat silently for a moment more, now only thinking about becoming a man. *What do I need to know? I need to know how to fight James Lee. I need to know how to fire two hundred pounds of human-shaped clay that's stuck in my closet. And I need to know . . .*

He looked up at Reb Chaim. "I need to know how to write the Hebrew word for God."

*The Word for God*

On the road home, both Sammy and his father were quiet. Soft rock was playing on the car radio, but neither of them leaned forward to turn the music off.

Sammy had no idea what his father was thinking about. Could be about some new pot he was making or about Skink, or about the bullying at school. Maybe it was only about the weather or the condition of the road they were on, still full of potholes from last year's tough winter.

But Sammy knew what was running through his own brain. The strange Hebrew letters that made up the word *Adonai*. God. Reb Chaim had shown them to him and made a first copy for him to trace without even asking why he wanted to know. Sammy had that first copy and all his own attempts on slips of paper in his pocket. He sat with his hand over his pocket to keep them safe. Those slips were all precious. Though he hadn't told Reb Chaim why he wanted to learn to write the name of God, he knew from the stolen book that one of the two ways to make the golem live—*animate* was the word the book's author used—was to place the Hebrew name of God on a slip of paper under the monster's tongue.

*Animate.* It had nothing to do with cartoons. Sammy had looked it up when he'd read the book the first time. It meant "to bring to life." *Funny word though*, he'd thought then. *Like animal. But without a mate.*

The other way was to write the name of God on the golem's forehead. *A sort of early Jewish tattoo*, he thought with a smile. But his Hebrew was too wobbly yet for that. *And what if I make a slip? A slip of the letters. Not a slip of paper.* And then he realized that anyone at school would be able to see letters on the golem's forehead: a dead giveaway. *Or a live one.* He giggled out loud. The slip of paper under the tongue would have to do.

"Sammy—you okay?"

He patted his pocket. "Fine, Dad, fine." He turned to look out the side window, his mind already back on the golem and the golem's tongue.

Of course, he had to make the head first.

And the tongue.

He stuck out his own tongue out, tried to look down and see it, but it didn't stick far enough out. So he pulled open the small mirror in the sun visor and stuck out his tongue again.

"Sammy, what *are* you doing? Feeling sick?"

What could he say—*Dad I wanted to see how a tongue is constructed*? That would lead to a conversation he definitely did *not* want to have.

"Maybe," he said, and smiled to himself. *This opaque stuff is really useful.*

"Then I'll get you home as soon as possible, and let your mother take your temperature." His father's foot slammed down on the gas pedal and Sammy lay back, eyes closed, as if this time he really was sick. Or tired.

He promptly fell asleep.

Sammy was awake for barely enough time to get from the car to the house and then went to his room and slept some more. Visions of the strange glyphs that made up *Adonai* danced through his dreams, turning into monstrous beasts with James Lee's face, and then morphing into dancing mermaid tattoos that all looked like Julia Nathanson. When the dream changed again, he was Dr. Frankenstein leaning over the monster, shouting, "He's alive! Alive!" Only when the monster sat up, he looked like Sammy's twin.

Sammy woke in time for dinner with his sheets drenched in sweat and his mother standing over him, concern written all over her face.

She felt his forehead before popping the thermometer in his mouth. Sammy lay still and waited for the thin beep. He didn't have to hear the verdict; he could tell by the worry lines on his mother's forehead what it was.

"Oh," he groaned, "now I really *am* sick."

His mother nodded, frowned, and patted him lightly on the head. "I'll make you some chicken soup for supper."

"Thanks, Mom." He almost slipped up and called her *Mommy*.

*Fevers always make me feel four years old.*

Then sighing, he rolled over and buried his face in the pillow so he wouldn't have to see the room spin . . .

And woke up three hours later to a thermometer in his mouth and a cold bowl of soup on his nightstand.

"Ugh," he said. Then, "Erg."

"I agree," his mother said, and checked the beeping thermometer. "Holding steady at one hundred and two."

"Ew."

"Guess you get some more time off from school."

"Hooray."

His mother smiled a little in the half-light of his table lamp. "Be careful what you wish for, Sammy." She handed him two ibuprofen tablets and a glass of water.

Sammy shrugged. It made his neck hurt. In fact, his whole body ached from the fever. "I guess."

"Get some more rest. Hopefully your fever will break overnight."

"Yeah. Hopefully." *It doesn't feel like it's going to be breaking anything but my spirit for a while*, he thought. But he drifted back to sleep thinking about the word *hopefully* and wondering what it looked like in Hebrew.

The alarm, which he'd forgotten to turn off, sounded promptly at one a.m., dragging Sammy out of a fever-induced dream where a headless clay god—that somehow still sported a long white beard—chased him through the school hallways. He tried to shake off the troubling image, but it just set his head pounding.

"The head!"

He had to make the head.

Eventually he'd get well and eventually have to go back to school. He needed the golem ready when that happened or he was dead meat. And Skink along with him.

Stumbling out of bed, his pajamas soaked from fever sweat, Sammy lurched to the closet and uncovered the golem. It loomed over him, five and a half feet of molded clay lacking only a head to make it whole and the name of God to make it live. In his fevered state, Sammy really believed it was going to work. But in his fevered state, he was nearly incapable of dragging a new block of clay from the closet to the bed. So he unwrapped the block on the floor of the closet, at the feet of the golem, and started to work right there. Spreading his tools around him, he began chopping and shaving, molding and smoothing, until he had an egg-shaped sphere.

"Hair?" he muttered. Then made a feverish decision: "Too much trouble." So he kept the top of the egg smooth, and concentrated on making eyes. After a few false starts he had a convincing pair of peepers. They were quite large, but so was the head. And the body.

"Golem, why are your eyes so big?" Sammy said in a high-pitched voice. He answered himself in a low growl. "The better to see James Lee coming, my dear."

*Wow! I* am *delirious!* he thought. Then mentally scolded himself: *Less talk. More clay.*

He added thick browridges to shade the big eyes and made the pupils more crescent than round, in the hopes that the similarity to cat's eyes would let the golem see well in the dark. "Darwin, do your work!" he whispered.

The nose insisted on being broad and flat, like a tribesman's, the ears slightly cauliflowered like Sammy had seen on the school's wrestling team coach.

He carved away some of the clay to make sharp cheekbones and a chin, first adding and then smoothing out a chin dimple made famous by a family of old actors. Then changing his mind, he put the chin dimple back in. He shaped the ears separately, and then stuck them on—he went with detached lobes—before finally coming around to the mouth.

Stumbling into the bathroom, he checked out his tongue again. Noticed the strange flap where it attached to the bottom of his mouth. Noticed that the tongue looked smooth at a distance, but up close it was a random, pitted landscape as pocked as the moon and bumpy as alligator skin. He studied it again and again before finally returning to his room and getting back to work again, figuring that if under the tongue was where the name of God went, then he'd better get the details right.

His fever was still raging as he starting digging into the head to make the open mouth. His eyes watered with hot fever tears that made the air seem to shimmer, which in turn made the golem's head seem to move. Its eyes appeared to follow his hands' movements, and he swore the golem's body was leaning farther over his left shoulder to get a better look at what he was doing.

*How can it see over my shoulder when I have its head at my feet?* In his fevered state, that seemed a reasonable question. *How can it move before I've had the chance to animate it?* Another good question. All of it he put down to his fever.

Sammy ignored the heat in his cheeks and went on hollowing out the mouth, forming a uvula at the back of what was now definitely a throat. He made teeth from scraps of clay—thirty-two in all. Luckily they'd studied the human body last year at his other school and the number of teeth had been on the final exam.

"The better to eat you with, my dear!" He chuckled softly.

After that was done, Sammy went over and over the tongue, taking a lot of breaks to stumble back to the bathroom mirror and stare at himself with his own tongue stuck way out, until he felt he had a reasonable copy of it in clay only proportionally larger. As he picked the finished tongue up to set it in the golem's gaping mouth, he shivered. And it wasn't just from the fever.

"Wow, a tongue sure is a huge, ugly thing!" He remembered his uncle Gerry who liked to eat tongue sandwiches. *Cow tongues must be humongous!* The thought made his stomach turn over, and for a moment he was afraid he was going to throw up.

"Golem won't like being decorated with puke!" he scolded himself.

Sitting for a moment more, he got control of his stomach, his thoughts, his sweaty hands. Then he smoothed the tongue into place inside the now toothy mouth, making sure there was room for the slip of paper that had to go there.

For a few anxious moments, he struggled to set the sizable noggin onto the golem's body. He had to wet some extra clay, then balance—rather dizzily—on a footstool while smoothing the wet clay to the creature's neck and shoulders to help hold everything in place. Luckily, the strokes formed natural-looking neck muscles and ligaments, and Sammy found himself wondering if that was how God had formed Adam's neck.

Then he started wondering that if he—as a Jew—didn't believe God's son was a carpenter, could he believe that God Himself was a potter?

*And what*—he asked himself—*would Darwin say?* The thought made him giggle.

"Your golem is totally un-evolved, son," he said aloud in a low voice, which occasioned another giggling fit.

Suddenly he realized how tired and sick he must be, with his mind leaping about, his hands shaking. *Maybe I should wait till tomorrow to take the final step.* But no, it was time, because the golem's neck was smooth and the head firmly in place, and the mouth was open with the tongue upturned, and all that was left was to write the name of God.

*Adonai.*

His hands shook so much that he knew he wouldn't be able to print the Hebrew word clearly. Still, he had the slips of paper.

*But where are they?*

Then he remembered—in his pants pocket.

*But where are the pants?*

Afraid his mother had already washed the pants—she was fast that way, washed glasses before you finished drinking, washed plates before you'd finished eating—

he rooted around in the clothes hamper but only found two pairs of dirty underpants and two T-shirts.

*Then where . . .?*

He turned and saw his pants at the foot of his bed.

*Thanks goodness Mom has been too busy to do the laundry!*

Fishing out the papers from the pocket, he smoothed them with his clay-pocked hands.

In the dim light from the closet he saw how wobbly his own Hebrew letters were compared to Reb Chaim's. He didn't dare chance the poor writing. Taking Reb Chaim's slip of paper, he placed it carefully under the golem's tongue. The huge, ugly, uplifted tongue.

"Live," he whispered, adding, "this Jew needs your help. Keep me safe." He thought a minute, adding, "Oh—and my friend Skink, too."

Then almost passing out with fever and exhaustion, he closed the closet door and went back to bed.

And dreamed that he was making a golem.

Sammy woke drenched in sweat but clearheaded. The fever had broken. Sitting up in bed, he tried to sort fevered memories from the dream images that still lingered.

He shook his head. *Whatever,* he thought, *it's* all *weird.*

Throwing off his blankets, he barely got one leg on the floor, when there was a knock on the door, and he scrambled back under the covers, making sure to tuck away his clay-spattered hands.

"Come in!"

His mother bustled in with a glass of water and a thermometer, and looked at him critically. "Well, now, don't you look a whole lot better!"

She put the water on his nightstand and popped the thermometer in his mouth. "Hardly need to take your temperature. I can tell your fever's broken." Putting her hands on her hips, she looked down at him. "I think it's time to go back to school, don't you?" She didn't wait for an answer, just spun around and marched to the closet. "Let's get you some clothes and get you off to school."

*Oh, God! Not the closet!*

There was nothing Sammy could do. He was in bed with a thermometer in his mouth, and before he could grunt or speak or jump out of bed to protest, she was at the closet and opening the door.

*I can't watch.* He turned his head away and squeezed his eyes shut, though he knew it was an infantile reaction. All he could do was wait for his mother to say, "Sammy? What is *that*?" That being a golem. And bits of clay. And a trashed closet. And . . .

In fact, he was terrified. Terrified what his mother would say in another second about his closet and what his father would say about all the wasted clay, and terrified that it would all lead to the discovery of his theft from Rabbi Chaim.

His thoughts kept him from realizing that one second had turned into two, and then three and four and five, and then Sammy realized that either his mother was too stunned to speak or something very strange was happening. Slowly, he turned his head back toward the closet and opened just one eye. His mother's back blocked his view of the closet as she stood peering into it, one finger tapping her cheek.

Sammy opened his other eye.

His mother reached out and snagged a shirt with bright stripes that he hated and some pants that would get him wedgied for life. He didn't say anything, though. Because, as she turned back with the clothes draped over her arm, he could see clearly into the closet.

*There's no golem in there!*

Sammy was too stunned to speak. He was too stunned to think. He lay transfixed, staring into the closet, as his mother took the thermometer out of his mouth and smiled at the normal reading. She puttered around his room for another minute and then said, "Okay, Sammy, dear. Get up and get dressed. Your dad's driving you to school and after that he's got a big order to fill. We won't be seeing him for days. I have a lunch date so am going out later and need to get stuff done here before going."

Sammy didn't answer. He was still staring at the

empty closet, trying to figure out where the golem had gone.

*Did I move it?* Could *I have moved it? Would I* remember *that? And how could it have moved? It hasn't been fired yet. And* . . . His thoughts and memories were all jumbled up.

"Sammy?" his mother said.

"Um . . . yeah. School. Up. Okay."

*Or had the whole thing just been a fever dream from first to last?*

His mother turned and was about to walk out, but then stopped in the doorway and looked over her shoulder. "Oh! I almost forgot. A friend of yours from school has stopped by to see how you're doing."

"Skink? He's out of the hospital?"

His mother shook her head. "No. Well, yes, Skinner is out of the hospital. Only stayed overnight. Been home five days now. But no, the friend is someone else, someone we've never met before. He's—" She stopped. Frowned. "Well, I hate to be so blunt, Sammy, but he's a strange-looking kid. Big for an eighth grader. And bald as an egg!"

"Um . . ." Sammy's mind was whirling, a thousand thoughts a second whizzing through.

*It worked!*

*It couldn't have.*

*There's got to be another explanation.*

*It's magic!*

*It's bunk!*

*Alopecia.*

"Alopecia?" his mother asked. He hadn't realized he'd spoken the last thought aloud. "You do know the oddest words, Sammy."

"Um . . ." *Where'd I come up with that one?* Then it hit him. They'd studied alopecia in the human body class, as well. "It's . . . it's hair loss that can occur at any age. My . . . um . . . *friend* suffers from it."

"Oh." She nodded. "I'm glad it's that. I thought it might be cancer. He doesn't look well. Sort of gray, if you know what I mean." She turned toward the door and this time did walk out, saying over her shoulder, "Get dressed. Your father and your friend are already sitting down for breakfast."

"Erp." It was hardly a response, but she took it as such and shut the door after her.

Sammy sat up. Pulled his hands out from under the covers and stared at them. They were pretty clean.

Put his feet on the floor. They held him up.

His mind was no longer whirring. In fact, it seemed entirely empty.

He put on the dorky pants one leg at a time. Then the striped shirt.

Plodding into the bathroom, he turned on the water and washed his face. The coolness felt grand. Afterward, he washed his hands, getting rid of the rest of the clay. He hoped the cool water would kick-start his brain, but if anything it numbed him even more.

Back in his room, he put on socks. Sat on the bed. Listened to his mother shout, "Sammy! Breakfast!" Finally, he stood, hiked up his pants, yanked down his shirt, and headed for the stairs.

And there, sitting at the kitchen counter, head and shoulders poking out from behind the basket of flowers and fruit Sammy's mother kept on the table, was the golem. The tall, broad-shouldered, gray-skinned, hairless golem. He was fully dressed in canvas pants, work boots, a tan V-neck T-shirt, and a Chicago Cubs baseball cap. Though where the golem had gotten those clothes, Sammy was never to know.

Sammy sat. "Hi . . . um . . . , Gully," he said, "nice to see ya."

The golem nodded.

"Had any breakfast yet?" Sammy asked, glad he'd given the creature teeth, though worried because he hadn't given it any internal organs, like a stomach or a colon. Or, for that matter, a . . . um . . . hole for food to exit from. "Or are you not hungry?"

"Not hungry," the golem said. Its voice was large. Flat. Uninflected.

*Uninflected*, Sammy thought, *as well as uninspected, undetected, and possibly unsuspected*. At least he hoped so.

"Nonsense, Gully—is that your name?" Sammy's mother said. "I've never known a boy your age who couldn't eat more."

"Gully," said the golem, smiling. The mouthful of teeth were the color of the clay.

"He's not much of a talker, Old Gully," Sammy put in quickly. He raced through his own cereal and banana so quickly, it felt as if it had all become a mass of clay in his belly.

*Tongue.* He remembered that enormous tongue he'd shoved into the golem's mouth just hours before, and all the banana and cereal threatened to return as quickly as it had gone down.

"I've noticed," Sammy's father said, who had been sitting behind the newspaper and not doing much talking himself.

"All done," Sammy said, putting down his napkin. "Let's go, Gully. Don't want to be late. I'm never late."

"I've noticed," said Gully. Again in that flat voice.

Sammy stood, the golem stood, and Sammy's mother stood, too. "Well, I've never seen you so eager to get to school, Sammy."

"I just don't want to miss any more," he answered, trying to keep his voice even, though not quite uninflected. "Or make Gully late. He's new to the school—and it wouldn't be a good start." He could feel his heart pitter-patting like mad, and hoped no one else could hear it. He knew that if he didn't get the golem away from the prying eyes of his parents, things might really spiral out of control.

As for the golem, so far he seemed to say only what he'd heard spoken. Maybe he needed a vocabulary lesson.

*But—I have to be careful*, Sammy told himself. *Careful what I do and what I say.* He'd been so intent on *making* the golem, he hadn't given any thought to what was suppose to come after.

"Come on, Gully. Time for school."

The golem grinned his big gray grin again. "I want a good start," he said, almost as if he was being as careful as Sammy.

They made a strange procession out to the car: Sammy's father, small but powerful, taking the lead with a steady march; then slight Sammy, not watching where he was going and almost tumbling onto the walk because he kept craning his neck around to look at the golem; and at the last Gully, whose long strides threatening to carry him past the other two.

His mother had insisted. "A new boy and a boy just back from having a fever? Of course Dad will drive you." She didn't mention the bullies, but Sammy suspected she was thinking about that, too, and he didn't protest.

Sliding into the backseat, he motioned Gully to sit next to him. The golem looked the car up and down and side to side before ducking his head low to slide in.

"Seat belts!" Sammy's father called.

Sammy leaned over and grabbed Gully's seat belt, stretching it nearly to its limit to get it around Gully's big frame, before clicking it into place.

"Seat belts?" Gully asked, raising an eyebrow.

"Seat belts to keep you safe," Sammy said, wondering

at the same time when he'd given the golem eyebrows. He couldn't remember doing it. Then he leaned back and grabbed his own seat belt. But before he could stretch it across his chest, Gully snatched it from his grasp, and with a motion that looked practiced—but obviously couldn't have been—whipped it around Sammy and clicked it into place.

"Seat belts," Gully said, with a satisfied nod. "To keep you safe."

Sammy smiled at him and Gully smiled right back.

*I wish I'd glazed those teeth white*, Sammy thought. But of course he'd never glazed anything without his father's help. And even if his dad hadn't noticed the enormous amounts of missing clay, he'd have surely figure out the kiln had been used at night—by the residual heat if nothing else.

*Residual*, he thought. *A good word. For a difficult moment. Trying to cover for a made-up creature who was created out of residual ideas and leftover clay. All gray.*

However, he didn't have to look at the offending teeth for long. As soon as Sammy's father got the car rolling down the driveway, Gully's smile disappeared into a tight-lipped frown and his eyes bugged wide. His whole body went tense, his arms bulging with ropy muscles and his grayish knuckles turning white where his hands grabbed the edge of the car seat.

But he only stayed that way for the briefest of moments. With a snort like an angry bear, he released the seat belt, leaned forward, his hands curling into alarmingly large fists. Then he sneered at the back of Sammy's father's head, pulled his right fist back, and—

"No!" Sammy screamed, and flung himself across the backseat at the golem.

"What? Did you forget something for school?" Sammy's father glanced in the rearview mirror. "And why are you hanging off your friend's arm?"

The golem was looking down at Sammy as if he wanted to know the answer to that last question, too.

"Um . . ." Sammy began uncertainly. "Gully here is a nervous rider." He patted the golem's arm. "He doesn't have a lot of experiences riding in *cars*." He patted the seat. "Cars." He patted it again. "Cars that help us get from one place to the other and are usually driven by my family that I love. And that I don't want hurt."

"What in the name of Thomas Wedgwood are you going on about?" Sammy's father demanded. "A nervous rider? Never been in a car? Is Gully Amish, or something?"

*Thank you, Dad!*

"Yes, exactly!" Sammy gushed. "Amish."

"Car," Gully said. "Amish."

Sammy plumbed his mind for everything he knew about the Amish.

*They don't use technology. They ride in wagons and raise barns. They have funny beards and even funnier names.*

Then he remembered the most important fact he'd gleaned from his extensive research into the Amish culture, which involved watching half of one old movie with the Indiana Jones guy and reading a couple of *Newsweek* articles in the bathroom.

"He's on his *rumspringa*," Sammy said.

"*Rumspringa?*" Sammy's father asked.

"I think that's the word."

"*Rumspringa*," Gully said confidently.

*At least* he *sounds like he knows what he's talking about!*

Sammy looked at the golem, "You want to explain, or should I?"

Gully gazed benevolently back at him. "You explain."

"When the Amish turn sixteen," Sammy said, "they're allowed to leave the church and explore the outside world before deciding whether they want to rejoin as adults."

*There*, Sammy thought, *I've exhausted my knowledge of the Amish.*

"Interesting," Sammy's father eyed Gully in the mirror. "He's sixteen? And in your class?"

*Ugh.* "Um, yeah. Apparently the Amish education system isn't all it's cracked up to be." *Double ugh.*

Sammy's dad chuckled. "Rumspringa. Sort of like an Amish bar mitzvah!"

"Bar mitzvah," Gully said cheerfully. "Rumspringa. Sort of like."

"Sort of like," agreed Sammy as he helped the golem put the seat belt back on. But inside, he was disgusted with himself. The creature he'd made had just tried to punch out his dad. *And now I'm spinning lie after ridiculous lie to protect him.* Sammy knew that if he got asked any more questions, the lies were going to start piling one on top of another until they inevitably collapsed into a big, stinking heap of untruth, with Sammy and whatever was left of his integrity, dignity, and self-respect crushed underneath.

For the first time that he could remember, Sammy couldn't wait to get to school. At least there, separated from Gully—who would surely be put in the remedial classes—he'd be safe. From the lies.

But once they were left off near the school, Sammy
remembered why he hated the place. There, in a row by
the front door, looking like a police lineup, stood James
Lee and the beat-em-up crew. They were hassling the
younger kids, hustling their milk money, and laughing
uproariously whenever one of the younger kids began
to cry.

"Gully," Sammy said, turning to the hulk by his side,
"time to earn your living. And by that, I mean *living*. As
in *life*! Okay?"

"Earn living," the golem said. "Okay."

But how much Gully really understood, Sammy
could only guess at.

They walked side by side up to the stairs.

"James Lee," Sammy tried to explain. "The big kid
on the left. He's the really bad one."

"Bad," the golem said. "Left." His head went back
and forth, surveying the whole crew.

Sammy pointed. "That's left. And that . . ." he
pointed to the other side, "is right. Got it?" *Honestly*, he
thought, *it's like trying to raise a kid. A huge, ugly, hulking,
bald kid.* "Oh, and turn your hat around so the front is

the back." He made a motion with his hand describing the hat and how to turn it.

"Okay." Gully said. "Got it."

*How* much was okay and *what* did he get, Sammy still hadn't a clue, but at least the golem turned the hat around so the brim was at the back.

"Not a complete dork now," Sammy muttered.

"Complete dork now," Gully echoed.

Side by side, they marched up the stairs.

Waiting at the top, James Lee smiled broadly. "Well, well, well—welcome back, Sammy GreenBug. Got any money to pay the toll?"

*Well, here goes nothing.* Sammy stopped, clenched his fists, and tried to give James Lee a manly stare. But he was still a step down and had to look way up, which was not a good angle.

Gully stopped, too. But even though Gully shared the step with him, Sammy noticed that James Lee had to look up to meet the golem's eyes. That lent Sammy courage.

"I think you mean pay the *troll!*" Sammy told James Lee. "And listen up, troll, I'm never paying you another dime ever again."

"That so?" James Lee sneered. "Who's your ugly friend?"

"His name is Gully and . . ."

"He related to you, GreenBug?" said Erik, the boy Ms. Snyder had said was smart but as far as Sammy could tell was only smart-alecky. "He a GreenBug, too? 'Cause with him I bet the BUG stands for Big Ugly Guy." He turned to James Lee. "Get it?" He started to spell it out, literally, and had gotten to the G when light seemed to dawn in James Lee's eyes.

"Yeah," James Lee said, smiling at Erik. "Big Ugly Guy."

"Yeah," the rest of the Boyz parroted, "Big Ugly Guy."

James Lee turned his attention back to Gully. "You don't want to hang around with losers, do you? Stick with us."

Gully shook his head. "I . . . I . . ." he stuttered.

*Oh, no,* Sammy thought. *Real bad time for my golem to get nervous.*

James Lee cackled at Gully's stuttering. "I . . . I . . . I . . ." He plastered an idiotic expression to his face, lips twisted up and eyes bugging out.

"I . . . I . . . I . . . Aye, aye, Cap'n!" He busted out laughing, and the Boyz joined in.

"I . . ." Gully went on as Sammy hung his head.

*I hope the toilet's been flushed recently,* Sammy thought. And then something else came to him. *Won't unfired clay dissolve in a toilet bowl?*

But Gully had already stopped stuttering, saying quite clearly, "I hang around the Sammy. He's tough for a little guy." He glanced at Sammy as if seeking approval of his sentence structure.

Sammy gave him a small smile and nodded as Gully turned back to James Lee who merely looked confused.

"Tough?" James Lee reached out to grab Sammy's shirt with his right hand. Sammy shrank back, but he needn't have bothered. Two hundred pounds of golem was suddenly between James Lee's big hand, and Sammy's shirt and Gully's even bigger hand was wrapped around James Lee's neck. Slowly, James Lee's face began to turn a rather brilliant shade of red. His hands banged ineffectively on Gully's chest.

"Get him," James Lee said in a strangled voice.

One of the Boyz—Brandon Overman—obeyed and leaped at Gully, but the golem seemed to just shrug and send him flying down the stairs. He managed to roll instead of tumble, which saved him from a cracked skull, but he didn't seem in a hurry to climb back up the stairs. None of the other Boyz jumped in.

Sammy—who was enjoying this way too much—
noticed that James Lee's face was turning from red
to blue, and his hands that moments ago had been
pummeling Gully's chest were now fluttering aimlessly.

"Better let go now, Gully," Sammy said.

"He's the really bad one," Gully said. "On the left."

James Lee's shoulders slumped. His arms dropped
to his sides.

"Let go now!" Sammy managed to keep his voice
*just* below a scream.

"Okay." Gully let go and James Lee collapsed to
the ground. *Now* his friends came to his aid, crowding
around him and glaring up at Gully. Brandon even tried
to tell Gully how lucky he was to have stopped when he
did. But even he didn't sound as if he believed it.

A small cheer went up from the few kids not already
inside the school. Then they hurriedly pushed past the
Boyz who stepped back to let them go through the door.

Sammy grabbed Gully by the hand. "Time for class."

"Class," Gully repeated.

As they followed the kids into the school, Sammy
smiled, thinking: *Victory!* His first ever against James
Lee. *First ever against anyone, actually.* He felt like a
Western hero who'd just survived a gunfight and was

riding into the sunset with his girl. He looked up at the big, gray golem who stared blankly at the group of boys he'd just backed down. *Well, close enough.*

Then, right before they got through the door, Sammy looked over his shoulder and told James Lee, in a passable imitation of the old-time movie star his father loved, John Wayne, "New sheriff in town, pilgrim. Better get used to it."

James Lee looked puzzled.

But then, thought Sammy, when he wasn't angry, he often looked puzzled, as if someone thinking differently than he did just didn't compute.

Giving James Lee no more thought, and pulling Gully after him, Sammy went into the school.

The first person to greet them was Julia Nathanson. She was grinning broadly. "That was awesome!" she said. "I watched through the window." She pointed to the hall window where a knot of younger kids was still gathered. "We were *all* watching. It was like a Western shoot-out. Who's your friend?" She looked pointedly at the golem.

"Gully," Sammy said. He was thinking about the hero riding off into the sunset with the girl. His voice cracked and sputtered, so he cleared his throat. Tried again. "Gully, this is Julia. She's one of the good guys."

"On the right," the golem said.

"Gully?" Julia asked. "What kind of a name is that?"

"Short for . . . um . . . Gulliver," Sammy said.

"Gulliver," Gully added. He was smiling and his gray teeth showed.

"Gulliver?"

"Well, it's . . . a family name." Sammy was almost trembling. More lies. "And well, that's the kind of name other kids can make fun of. Like a cousin of mine who was going to be named Adam Scott Silverman until they figured out the initials and . . ."

Julia had to bite her bottom lip to keep from laughing, before saying, "You're making that up."

"Am not." Sammy let out the breath he'd been holding. The story about his cousin Adam, at least, was absolutely true.

"Then they shouldn't have named him Gulliver," Julia said, her head nodding toward Gully. "It's *absolutely* going to be the school joke."

"Don't tell," Sammy said.

Gully added, "Don't tell."

Julia put her finger to her lips.

Gully did the same.

And—just to be on the safe side—Sammy did, too.

At that moment, the first bell rang and Sammy, dragging Gully to the left, started down the corridor to his homeroom. Julia's homeroom was on the right.

But before she'd even got a few steps down the hall, she turned and called back, "Sammy?"

He turned so quickly, he almost fell over, and Gully's hand shot out to steady him.

"I'd like to be part of the band. With you and Skinner."

"Skinner?" His heart was beating like a drum. "Drum." He said it out loud.

"No, silly." She shook her head and her dark hair waterfalled around her long face. "Violin. I play the violin."

"Sure," Sammy said. And, as if his tongue had suddenly developed an echo pedal, he said it two more times. "Sure. Sure."

"I fiddle around. Let's talk at lunch," she said. Then added—before disappearing through the door of her homeroom—"That's a joke."

"Drum," Gully said.

Slowly, Sammy turned to him. "What?" His head was still filled with the idea of talking to Julia Nathanson. In the band. At lunch. Sitting with Julia Nathanson. At lunch.

"Drum," Gully said again. "Silly—I play drum."

"You don't even know what a drum is," Sammy told

him, and pulled him into homeroom. But suddenly, Sammy remembered the way Gully had slammed James Lee and the Boyz. Beaten on them. *Like a drum.*

*That's not a bad idea at all.* He'd never considered a drummer for the band.

Sammy had a story ready for the teachers when they asked about Gully: *He's a visiting cousin from Europe who is here to learn to speak English, and he can't stay home alone while my parents are at work.*

He knew it wasn't a particularly *good* story. It was full of enough holes to be a golf course. And if anyone thought to confirm this with his parents, he'd be in serious trouble. But it would explain the way Gully talked, if not his looks. And if any of them asked Gully where in Europe he lived, he'd probably answer, "Europe, silly," but it was all Sammy had come up with. *Maybe I'll say "Middle Europe,"* he thought, not exactly sure where Middle Europe was. *Except, probably somewhere . . . well . . . in the middle.* But his parents often talked about it because it was where their ancestors came from, before they lived in Hartford. Long before.

However, the thought of Ms. Holsten interrogating him in front of the entire homeroom class had Sammy chewing on his fingernails. The taste was awful because there was enough clay still embedded in them to make a meal, but still he chewed.

He introduced Gully to Ms. Holsten as she sat at her desk.

"Um, my cousin Gully. Gully Greenburg. From Middle Europe," he said. "Gully, this is Ms. Holsten."

"Poland? Slovenia? Czech Republic?" Ms. Holsten asked brightly.

"Czech Republic," Sammy said, having no idea which one would be best, just relieved that she'd given him three choices.

Gully nodded. "Check," he said. "Republic."

The Holstein nodded again, almost cowlike. Sammy was surprised that she didn't moo as well. "Welcome, Gully."

*Why isn't she saying anything more?* Sammy thought, biting a hangnail so short that it started to bleed. *She has to be curious about where he comes from in the Czech Republic. And what grade he's in. And why he's so gray.*

Then he had another thought—biting the hangnail again—*why did I ever think making a golem was a good idea. It's a terrible idea.*

But whether it was some magic of the golem's, or

Ms. Holsten's assumption that Sammy-the-Good-Kid must have the proper permissions to bring in a visitor, she made no mention again of Sammy's big, gray cousin except to have them get an extra chair and desk from the back of the room and sandwich it between Sammy's desk and Jason Fredericks, the goofy kid with the Coke-bottle glasses who sat on his right.

Ms. Holsten turned out to be the only real hurdle, because all of the teachers seemed to automatically assume that the teacher before them had cleared the visitor. Sammy only had to say that Ms. Holsten had said it was okay and that—it turned out—was the end of it. He'd even been ready to avoid lying outright by saying something like, "Ms. Holsten didn't say it wasn't okay." But he never had to resort to that new lie.

In fact, he'd gnawed his nails down to nubs for nothing.

With James Lee put in his place, and Gully looking like he'd be allowed to stick around, Sammy should have been nice and relaxed by lunchtime.

*Lunchtime.*

*With Julia Nathanson*

But apparently *that* was the thing he worried about

the most. Including the fact that he could quite possibly have a heart attack by sitting too close to her.

Or embarrass himself by letting out a fart during a lull in the conversation. If there *was* any conversation.

Or spilling lunch down his front. Or even worse— spilling lunch down hers.

Still, the one thing he knew he wasn't going to do any more damage to were his fingernails. He no longer had any.

*Lucky I play clarinet and not guitar.*

Sitting up straight in his chair, Sammy tried to listen to what Mr. Lippincott, the science teacher, was talking about. Neurons. Or protons. Or some such *ons.*

*I have to look relaxed.* He must have said it aloud, because Gully repeated in his flat voice, "Look relaxed."

The boy next to him, a pencil-thin geeky kid who knew all about science and not much else, broke out into giggles the way some kids break out in acne.

Sammy gave him a disgusted look and said, "Yeah, Gully—though in America we say: 'Look cool. Calm. Collected.'"

And then the bell rang for lunch.

Sammy stood, his knees suddenly shaking.

Gully stood and put a comforting hand on Sammy's

shoulder. They walked that way down the hall and to the lunchroom looking like two blind guys helping one another.

Julia Nathanson was already sitting at Sammy's table, looking—Sammy thought—cool, calm, collected. He could have pointed that out to Gully, a live vocabulary lesson, but it would have meant opening his mouth and letting real words, rather than a deep sigh, come out. Sammy simply didn't think he could manage it.

Instead, he gulped, and went right to the lunch line, though ordinarily he'd have taken off his backpack and left it at the table first. *Anything,* he thought, *to delay sitting down.* Which was decidedly odd since what he wanted to do—more than anything else in the world—was to sit down next to Julia.

He showed Gully how to take a tray and choose between mystery meat or "snap" sandwiches, which was what everyone called the toasted cheese sandwiches that were so hard, they could be snapped in two. And how to choose between green beans cooked until they were as gray as Gully or a small salad, somehow equally gray. And then there were the containers of different kinds of milk: whole, one percent, chocolate.

Gully took it all, slopping it onto his plate as if he could really eat the stuff, then carried both trays over to the table with one hand, an amazing feat.

Then finally—with nothing more to throw between himself and Julia—Sammy had to sit down next to her. He *had* to. His knees had suddenly become so weak, it was sit-or-fall-over time. He thought he might actually be having a heart attack.

There was a long, difficult silence, and then Sammy said to Julia, "This is my . . . um . . . cousin."

"Not much of a family resemblance," Julia replied.

Gully said to Julia. "I am Gully. The cousin. From Check."

"Check?" Julia sounded puzzled.

"Czech Republic," Sammy said. "He's gray from lack of sun and a condition called alopecia. He doesn't speak a lot of English, and he is the drummer in the band." And having divested himself of all of his conversation openers at once, Sammy fell silent again.

"Hi, Gully," Julia said. "Again."

"Again," Gully said, and nodded his head.

Only then did Sammy remember the conversation they'd had in the hall about Gully's name. *This is worse,* he thought, *than farting or spilling food, or* . . . Maybe the heart attack was a good idea. He wondered if a person could just will his heart to give out.

"The drummer?" Julia said. "That's great. Like I said, I want to be in the band, too. Can I try out?"

"Try out . . ." Sammy repeated, now sounding quite a bit like Gully, his voice flat and much too loud.

"You try out," Gully said. "Look cool." He grinned his gray grin. "We say that in America."

Julia laughed. It sounded like tinkling bells.

Sammy resisted slapping his forehead with his hand, but only just. *I can't believe I just thought "Tinkling bells!"*

"So can I try out?" Julia asked again.

Sammy nodded. He nodded so vigorously, he hoped his neck muscles were strongly attached. If his head fell off, he didn't know what he would do then.

They ate the rest of the meal in silence. Julia because she'd gotten what she wanted. Sammy because he had nothing sensible or amusing or interesting left to say. And Gully because without something to echo, he couldn't talk. And of course, though he ran his fork around and around the things on his plate, and even once held a forkful up to his mouth, Gully didn't actually eat any of it.

If Julia had asked why, Sammy was ready with an answer. He was going to say, "He's religious. Food's not kosher. That's Jewish for not holy." But she never said a word.

Nobody—not any of their classmates or the James Lee crew—disturbed the silence until the bell rang. The three of them stood.

"At last," Sammy said.

"At last," Gully parroted.

"Can I try out after school?" Julia asked.

"I . . . I have He . . . Hebrew lessons. For my b . . . bar mitzvah," Sammy stuttered.

"Cool. I was bat mitzvahed this past summer," Julia said. "We'll do it tomorrow then." Tray in hand, she walked away.

*Julia's Jewish?* Sammy was stunned. He guessed they must be the only two in the school. *What are the odds . . .?*

"I have Hebrew lessons?" asked Gully when Julia had disappeared through the door.

"Sure," Sammy said. "Why not."

"What are Hebrew lessons?"

This time Sammy didn't answer, though he was thinking that English lessons would probably make more sense for Gully.

*Though nothing . . . nothing makes any sense at all any more.*

*Gully and the Rabbi*

The rest of the school day ran smoothly, if you didn't count Gully pushing a seventh-grade girl who came over to shake Sammy's hand in the hall, or intercepting a dodgeball heading for Sammy's middle, growling at Mr. Nolan for slamming his hand down on Sammy's desk when he was admonishing the class. (Though *admonishing*, Sammy admitted, was a pretty cool word.)

Yeah, if you didn't count those, Sammy thought, things went pretty smoothly. Of course, Sammy spent a lot of time apologizing for his Czech cousin who was— or so Sammy said—brought up under a dictator and so thought anyone trying to touch his cousin or get too close or even looking crosswise at Sammy was sort of trying to hurt him. And best of all, it was all true, except for the Czech part. And the dictator part. And leaving out the golem part, which no one would have believed anyway.

Still, it ended up being a good thing because the word got around the school fast enough, and for the last period, everything really *did* sail along.

When the last bell sounded, Sammy retrieved his homework books from his locker and was just turning around to look for Gully, who he'd told to stand in the corner of the hall by the window and count birds. Gully was obeying orders, a big gray presence staring out at a couple of crows, when a lovely lilting voice called Sammy's name.

Turning, Sammy saw Skinner's mother coming down the hall toward him, her arms filled with books.

"Mrs. Williams!" he cried. "How's Skink?"

"Desirous of getting back to school. And your band," she said. "Though it may be a day or two more."

*Desirous. What a great word!* Sammy thought. Aloud he said, "Well, tell him I'm *desirous* of visiting him."

"Come this evening after dinner," Mrs. Williams said. "He could use the help with his homework." She reached into her pocketbook, which meant first putting the books on the floor. "Here's a card with our address on it. Your mother can call me to make certain of the invitation."

"I will! I will!" And then a gray blur caught his eye as Gully raced over to investigate this latest threat.

"Gully," Sammy said quickly, "this is a *good* friend's mother." He hoped the emphasis on good would get through, and it must have because Gully slowed down. Sammy sighed, then said, "Um, Mrs. Williams, this is my cousin Gully from Czech Republic. He's going to be the drummer in our band. Can he come, too?"

"I come, too?" Gully said, stooping and picking up the books and handing them to her, at the same time giving her a gray smile.

"Of course. Of course," she said, a bit startled at his sudden appearance.

*Or maybe*, Sammy thought, *just startled by his appearance.* But either way, she was too polite to say anything. *Which is nice, because I'd like to stop lying to people for at least a minute or two today.* And sighing audibly, Sammy stuffed his books into his backpack and headed for the door.

"Your Amish friend going to come to Hebrew lessons with you, Sammy?" his father asked as soon as they hopped in the car.

"Yes, please," Sammy said, and as usual Gully echoed, "Yes, please."

*I'm almost getting used to it.*

"And we've been invited to Skink's after dinner. Gully's going to be the drummer in our band. And Julia Nathanson's going to fiddle around."

"Julia? So I know her?"

"She's . . . um . . . a friend." He hoped his father didn't look in the rearview and notice him blushing.

"Friend. She fiddles around," said the golem. "A good one. On the right. That's a joke."

Sammy's father glanced at Gully in the mirror. "Sounds like you've got a whole band now. When's the first rehearsal?"

*Rehearsal? I guess it's more than just an idea now that Gully and Julia are on board.* Sammy's mind was suddenly full of all the little things he'd ignored up to this point. *Where will we practice? Can Julia play klezmer? Or jazz? If she can't, will I let her in the band anyway?* He blushed at how dumb that sounded. Of course he was going to let Julia in the band. *And—oh, God—how are we going to get Gully a drum kit?*

He didn't say any of this out loud, of course. "As soon as Skink's ready, I guess."

"There should be room in the basement if you clean it up some."

*Well, that's at least one question answered. Though maybe not the biggest.* "Thanks, Dad."

After that, *which went about as well as it could*, Sammy thought, his dad, asked how school was today, and they settled into small talk about classes and grades with Gully echoing the occasional word or phrase. Then Sammy asked about how the pots were coming along, and his dad broke into a long explanation about form following function or some such, which Sammy half listened to and Gully repeated a bit of.

Soon enough, though, they quieted down and stared out their respective windows. Sammy knew his father would be thinking about pot design.

He'd no idea what Gully was thinking, or even if golems *could* think.

*Which leaves me to worry about the golem.*

The three of them remained that way, gazing out their own windows, deep in whatever passed for thinking, until twenty-five minutes later when they pulled into the synagogue parking lot.

"*Shalom aleichem*," Reb Chaim said as they walked in. "Peace be with you."

Sammy, his father, and Gully all answered, "*Aleichem shalom.*"

*All of them.*

Sammy's father glanced curiously at Gully who was grinning grayly, but Sammy was used to the golem repeating things. *So he just switched the words around this time*, he thought. *So what?*

Reb Chaim, however, sure seemed surprised. His eyes went wide, taking in Gully's height, his bald head, his gray grin. The rabbi breathed, "*Barukh atah Adonai, Eloheinu, melekh ha'olam.*"

Gully nodded gravely and answered, "*Oseh ma'asei v'reishit.*"

"Gully knows Hebrew?" Sammy's father asked. "I thought he was Amish."

"Um . . ." Sammy said.

Reb Chaim shook himself and stood. "Mr. Greenburg, I need to speak with Samson immediately."

Sammy stepped forward, and Gully stepped with him, like a shadow.

"Alone," Reb Chaim said.

Gully looked at Sammy, his big gray fists clenched tight. "It's okay, Gully," he said, softly. "Just stay here. I'll be right back." Then he followed Reb Chaim into the sanctuary.

As soon as the door shut, Reb Chaim sat down on one of the benches and patted the seat next to him.

Sammy sat down tentatively, wondering what this was all about, though he was sure he knew. He didn't have to wait long.

Reb Chaim leaned toward him and nearly spat out his words. "What have you done, boy?"

"I . . . um . . ." Sammy decided that he was getting real sick of the word *um.* "Um . . ." *Doesn't seem to stop me from using it all the time.*

"Did you think that making a golem by a learned rabbi was an idle tradition?" Reb Chaim's normally pleasant face was almost purple with anger. "It was to avoid that very kind of abomination!" He pointed to the door they'd just come through. "That louring gray presence in the shul's hallway. That brutal clay animation. That . . ." He stood, started to walk about, his nervous energy seeming to spark out of his fingertips.

Sammy's hands—all on their own—began to wrangle together. He even ignored the word "louring" which he didn't know, and looked down at his hands, his mind blank. Then he looked up into Reb Chaim's angry face. "Well, I didn't think it would actually *work.* I mean—that's fairy-tale stuff, right?"

"Does that creature *look* like a fairy tale to you? Gray as clay, cold eyes, colder heart, with only one thing on its mind."

*Actually two things*, Sammy thought. *The other being drumming.* He knew better than to say that out loud. Looking down again at his hands, he willed them to be still. "I used the thing you wrote. You know—on that slip of paper. I couldn't write it well enough myself."

That stopped Reb Chaim's tirade. "I'm an idiot for not realizing what you wanted it for," he said, then glanced over at his bookcase. "I suppose you stole my book, as well."

"I was going to bring it back," Sammy said softly. "Next week. Definitely." He didn't mention having copied it. "Listen, Rabbi. I've been teased, called names, been beaten up, had my head shoved into the toilet. And I know we Jews are supposed to suffer in silence, but I'm sick of it. For the first time in like, ever, I had a good day at school today. A *good* day!" *What was the really cool word Reb Chaim had used? Oh, yeah—abomination.*

"Abomination or not, that made it worth the agony of making the golem. And it wasn't real easy, you know? I had to do it in my closet."

Reb Chaim's eyes softened. "You said that last time. That your head had been shoved in a toilet."

"More times than I want to remember. Well, maybe like seven. All right, *actually* seven. I counted." He stood. Trying to talk to the pacing rabbi was hard enough, but at least they could be eye to eye.

As if to balance their positions, Reb Chaim sat down again. Put his head in his hands. He was silent for a long moment, and Sammy knew better than to say anything more.

"Sit down, Samson." This time Sammy didn't and Reb Chaim didn't press the issue. He looked up. "I know the temptation power holds out to the powerless. And I know to what ends they'll go to get it." Now Chaim was staring off into space. "I worked for the Mosaad, Sammy."

"What's that?"

"A secret government organization in Israel that sometimes does bad things for a good cause."

"You mean like the CIA here?"

Reb Chaim nodded and looked back at Sammy, his

eyes clouded, as if recalling something awful. "I've seen things no one ever should. Then very softly, he added, "Done some, as well."

"Like what?" Sammy asked.

"Like working with a unit of golems we were developing as our first line of defense against our many enemies." Reb Chaim's face got misty with the memory. He closed his eyes.

"And . . ." Sammy leaned forward.

"And they turned on us when they thought *we* were the enemy. As golems always do. Though we thought we'd discovered the secret to stop that from happening." He shuddered, as if with cold. "I will say no more. The rest is between me and . . ." his eyes opened, looked up as if he could see through the ceiling. "But know this: on every Yom Kippur, I remember what I saw and did there in Rehovot, and I try to forgive myself. And every single year I fail."

*It must have been something pretty bad.* And then Sammy thought: *But Gully's not like that. I won't ever let him get like that. He listens to me.*

Reb Chaim stood, all nervous energy again. "Trust me, Samson, this will *not* end well. Your 'one good day' will turn into a thousand bad ones. Ask the prophet

Jeremiah. Ask Rabbi Loew. Ask me! A golem knows no right or wrong; it knows only enemy or friend. That is a duality that leads to only one thing—the grave. Right now you think you know who is enemy, who is friend; which is good, which is bad. But for how long will such a thing be true?"

"I don't know," Sammy said. It seemed to be the answer the rabbi wanted to hear.

"That's right!" Chaim snarled. "Because you know *nothing* about golems."

"Then *tell* me about them!" Sammy said. "How does it work? Why was I able to make one? Is there more to it than just *Adonai*? Does the golem have special powers? Do *you*?"

Reb Chaim held up his hand, and Sammy stopped babbling. "Samson, any Jew can make a golem, but not all know how. And most of us who do know how choose not to abuse that kind of power. Anymore." He smiled briefly, sadly, more like an emoticon than an actual smile. "And also, most of us are lousy potters. If you made this thing without help, at least you have that much talent, if not sense."

"No one helped me," Sammy admitted.

"Good," the rabbi said.

"But there must be more to it than that," Sammy said. "I *have* to know more!"

Reb Chaim's smile disappeared. "You only need to know this, Samson: Remove the name of God from this creature's forehead, from its mouth."

Head down, Sammy whispered, "Mouth." He wasn't sure Reb Chaim even heard him for the rabbi was in full cry.

"Rid yourself of him now. This very moment. This very day. Or I promise you that along with destroying your enemies, that creature will destroy all you hold dear."

"But . . ."

"No buts! Finish him off, Samson. As soon as possible. You're the only one who can. Do not return here for lessons or even enter this sanctuary again until you do." Reb Chaim folded his arms across his chest and stared at Sammy for three long seconds before very pointedly turning away. "And send me back my book." His voice was soft, sad, almost defeated.

Sammy stood and walked out of the room. Rabbi Chaim didn't try to follow him.

Gully was standing just where Sammy had left him, but his dad was nowhere in sight.

"*Shalom aleichem,*" Gully said.

"There's nothing shalom or peaceful about today at all," Sammy told him. "You've been grounded and maybe worse. And me—I've been royally reamed out by the rabbi and kicked out of Hebrew school."

He opened the front door of the synagogue and saw his dad leaning against the car, making some drawings. *Probably of new pots.* Expecting Gully to say something, he looked back. But Gully—his gray hands once again balled into enormous gray fists—had already started purposefully toward the sanctuary where Rabbi Chaim sat alone and unprotected.

"No, Gully" Sammy shouted. "No! Come back. We're going home."

"Rabbi is on the left?"

"The rabbi is on the right," Sammy said. "He *is* right, I guess. But it's not his head being dunked in the toilet."

Gully hesitated, slowly unballed his fists, even more slowly turned. "Going home," he said. "*Aleichem shalom.* Peace be with you, rabbi on the right." He followed Sammy out the door.

It was a quiet ride home after Sammy told his father that Reb Chaim had canceled class for today and answered the inevitable "Why?" with a shrug.

"I wish he'd called," Sammy's dad said. "This was a long ride for nothing." His right hand slapped on the steering wheel.

Staring out the window, Sammy ignored his father's pique, and instead thought hard about what Reb Chaim had said. *Were there really golem units? Did they look like Gully? How else would Rabbi Chaim have known immediately what Gully is? And what was the bad thing that the rabbi had to think and pray about it every Yom Kippur, the Jewish Day of Atonement.*

Ignored, Gully began tapping on the back of the front seat. The sounds were first like Mr. Greenburg's angry rhythms, then they morphed into some strange vicious syncopation.

The drumming pushed into Sammy's thoughts, and he looked over his shoulder at Gully who was staring intently at his own fingers as they tapped and tattooed through another measure. *Yeesh*, Sammy thought, *that might be in 11/16. I bet he'll make a* really *good drummer, especially for a klez jazz fusion band.* And then he bit his lower lip. *Which makes it* really *too bad that I have to get rid of him.*

Suddenly Sammy realized he'd decided. The stuff Reb Chaim had said was just too scary. He couldn't have a golem running amok and killing people. *I'll do it after dinner tonight, before I go to Skink's. Take him up to my room and . . .*

Sammy shivered. *After dinner.* He didn't want to think any more about it. So, leaning his head against the window, he let the outside world blur into meaninglessness as it sped by.

They pulled into the driveway and Sammy's father was out the door almost before the car stopped moving. Waving his hand, he called, "Got to get into the studio with these new drawings! I think I've got something good here."

Sammy trudged around the car to let Gully out because the golem hadn't gotten the hang of the door handle yet. He hesitated for a moment and looked down at Gully. From this angle, Gully seemed almost childlike, his large features a little soft and unformed, his expression guileless.

*This isn't going to be easy.* Before Sammy could open the door, he heard a chuckle from the end of the driveway. Looking up, he took an involuntary step back.

James Lee stood there with three of his Boyz, all holding on to their bicycles.

"Hey, Green-bug," James Lee said, smiling. "How long is your Big Bug cousin in town for? 'Cause as soon as he leaves, you're getting what your pal Stink got." The smile vanished, replaced by a sneer. "Only worse."

Sammy gulped. His face lost color. Clearly the fact that no one had arrested the crew for beating up Skink had only made them bolder.

Seeing the frightened look on Sammy's face, Gully began scrabbling at the door handle to get out of the car. Sammy leaned against the door.

*Not that I can hold it shut against him if he figures out the handle,* he thought. *But I don't want anyone getting killed.* He glanced up at James Lee and the Boyz. *Especially me.*

"Um . . . James? Can we talk about this?" Sammy knew the answer to this already, and felt like an idiot for saying it. An idiot and a wimp. If he was going to rid himself of the golem, he needed to take charge of this situation. And now. So he took a deep breath and added, "That is if your peanut brain isn't mashed too hard with the jelly minds of your friends." He took a deep breath. "That's what the kids will call you tomorrow in school: PB&J Brains."

James Lee got a strange, angry look on his face. Clearly he was the designated name caller and Sammy should have known better. But Sammy's threat—if it could be called that—had had an unexpected consequence.

"See ya around the school yard, Little Bug," James Lee said, before vaulting on to his bike, turning a hard left, pulling a high wheelie, with his three leather-clad minions pedaling in his wake. It was meant to look spectacular and frightening but to Sammy it just looked pathetic.

*I did it!* Sammy thought before a second thought hit him. *But for how long?*

"The bad one!" Gully snarled, suddenly materializing by Sammy's side.

That was when Sammy realized that Gully had figured out the door on the other side and gotten out of the car. *I was too caught up in mouthing off at James Lee to hear him.* He sighed. *James Lee must have seen Gully, though. That's why he ran off.*

Beside him, Gully sniffed the air like a bloodhound getting the scent. "The bad one on the left!"

"No, Gully. Let him go. Let them all go. For now." Even though he would have loved to set Gully on the trail, Sammy couldn't allow the golem to maul anyone on his parents' doorstep.

*Maul. As in bang, bash, batter, beat, knock around.*

They'd just started toward the house when Sammy had another thought: *If I get rid of Gully now, I'm going to die. But if I keep him around, someone else is going to die.* He shook his head. *Maybe this is what Reb Chaim was worrying about.*

He corralled Gully into the house. All the while the golem kept looking back angrily at the last place James Lee and company had been before disappearing down the road. His fists curled and uncurled, but he made no move to follow the gang.

"Maybe Reb Chaim is wrong," Sammy whispered as he walked Gully up to the front door.

"Reb Chaim is wrong," Gully said, turning his head so far around to look over his shoulder at Sammy, it looked as if it might snap off. But of course it didn't.

"No, no . . ." Sammy assured him. "Reb Chaim is a good guy."

"On the right." The golem nodded.

"And probably *in* the right, too," Sammy murmured, thinking: *Things should be okay if I keep a* really *close eye on Gully. Or distract him. Sort of like Aunt Betsy and Uncle Ad*

*distract their two-year-old who* . . . here Sammy chuckled
. . . *pound for pound is as destructive as a golem.*

Now Gully was stopped at the door and began
banging his fingers rhythmically against it. But it was
drumming, not anger.

*I* can *control him.* Sammy nodded to himself. *I'm*
sure *I can.* He turned the knob and Gully watched with
interest. Then they went in.

Skink was looking much better. Not back to his old self,
but much better.

"Hey," Sammy said. They were up in Skink's room,
Skink reclining on the bed. Gully plopped down cross-
legged on the floor, and Sammy sat in front of a couple
of Skink's textbooks at his desk. They were there to do
homework, after all. "You don't look nearly as . . ."

"Gray?" Skink said, looking at Gully. "Like your
cousin? I don't mean to be, like, impolite," he said to
Gully, "but you don't look good, dude."

"Alopecia," Gully said, "and lack of sun, dude."

*Well,* Sammy thought. *At least I don't have to lie about
Gully anymore. He's doing just fine on his own.* "Let's get
back to algebra, Skink."

"Nah," Skink said. "Let's get back to the band!"

"Well, Dad says we can practice in my basement. And Gully, here, is going to be our drummer."

"Here is the drummer," Gully said predictably. He gave Skinner his biggest gray smile. His fingers pounded a wobbly beat on the floor.

"All right! What kind of kit do you have?"

"What kind of kit?"

Sammy cut in. "He doesn't have a drum kit yet. Not here. It's . . ." he thought quickly, "back where he used to live. His parents sold it. Too bulky to bring across the ocean. They're from the Czech Republic." *Here I go lying again*, he thought. *And to my best friend, this time.* "He'll need to get a new one. We'll probably go to Mr. Grambling's music store tomorrow. The one on Market Street? Do you know it?" He wondered dismally how he could pull that off. He had about six dollars in his old piggy bank and maybe a hundred in his bank account. He guessed a drum kit cost a whole lot more than that.

Gully nodded. "Need to get a new one."

"Awesome! And of course I know Grambling's. It's the best! First thing we looked for when we got here—a good music store. And practicing in your basement is awesome. It's already, like, set up for music. Long as

Gully's drum kit isn't a big one, we should have room for the three of us." He took a deep breath as if the galloping words themselves had exhausted him.

"The *four* of us," Sammy said carefully. "I told Julia . . . Julia Nathanson she could join." He said it all in a rush so he wouldn't stumble on her name. "If that's okay?"

"It's, like, *more* than okay." Skink no longer seemed exhausted. He held his fist out for Gully to bump, but the golem just stared at it, considering.

*Or, perhaps, judging whether it's a threat,* Sammy thought.

Having noticed nothing strange in Gully's expression, Skink continued. "We've got a real band now!"

In case the golem was getting the wrong idea about that fist, Sammy gave Skink a quick fist bump.

Just as if he were a cartoon character, Gully looked like a lightbulb had suddenly gone off above him. "Oh," he said, "awesome!" and gave Skink a fist bump, too, one hard enough to rock Skink back against his pillow.

"Not so rough, Gully," Sammy cautioned quietly. "He's one of the good guys."

"On the right," Gully said, nodding.

Skink grinned broadly. "We're all the good guys here."

"And a real band," Gully added.

*Well*, Sammy thought, *at least* most *of us are real.*

"She plays violin, right?" Skink said, less a question than an afterthought.

"Fiddle," Gully repeated. "She fiddles around. That's a joke."

"The first time it's funny," Sammy told him. "The second time passable. The third time it's . . . "

"Awesome!" Gully roared.

Sammy was going to say "stupid," but left it unsaid.

Skink furrowed his brow. "Fiddles can be jazz or country or classical. But can a fiddle be klezmer?"

Sammy smiled. "It's *very* klez."

"Sweet." Skink held out his fist to Gully and this time there was no hesitation.

*Bump*

"A real band," Gully said again, adding as if it was some kind of blessing, "Real sweet." He grinned his gray grin. "Awesome!"

"And now . . ." Sammy nodded at Skink. "Now for some *real* algebra."

Skink reached for a piece of paper on his bedside table. "Not so fast, Mr. Bug."

"Mr. Bug," repeated Gully, and for no apparent reason started to laugh. It was a creaky kind of laugh, as if he hadn't practiced it enough.

"I had a lot of time to think at the hospital," Skink said. "You wouldn't believe how awful TV is during the morning. And I came up with the lyrics to a new song for us to play. Of course there's no music yet. My hands weren't quite ready for that. But I thought—if you liked it—you could write the tune." He looked at the paper and began to read out loud:

Soul Power, Klez Style
*I've been up and I've been down,*
*I've been beaten all around.*
*I've been kicked upon the ground.*
*Power!*

Stopping a minute, he looked up. "It's supposed to start like an old black spiritual. My dad's really, like, into that. And of course, I really *was* kicked around."

"Got it," Sammy said.

"Power," Gully added, nodding his head.

"Read the rest."

Sammy sat down at the bottom of Skink's bed and read outloud:

> *I've been hit and I've been named.*
> *I've been dissed and shook and shamed,*
> *And it's all a power game.*

"Power!" Again, Gully's voice was a rumbling roar.

Skink grinned broadly and went on. "Here's the chorus. Didn't have time to write it all down yet."

> *You don't have it,*
> *So you want it.*
> *Once you get it,*
> *Then you flaunt it.*
> *If you use it,*
> *Don't abuse it,*
> *You will lose it . . .*

At that point, all three of them shouted: "POWER!"

Sammy's arm shot up in a fist salute. Skink's followed. And last of all, and on the right beat, so did Gully's.

There was a knock on the door. Mrs. Williams's voice called out tentatively, "Everything all right in there?"

"All right," Gully shouted.

And suddenly Sammy knew it really *was* all right. Gully wouldn't have to be dis-animated. The Boyz would be controlled. And Sammy and his friend— *friends!*—would have a band. He grinned nonstop.

For a long minute the three boys were silent, just as if they were all having the same thoughts.

Then Skink said, "There's, like, another two verses."

"Let's have them," Sammy said.

"Power!" Gully's fist went up in the air again.

Reciting from memory, his eyes closed, Skink began:

> *Take the power in your hands.*
> *It's your turn to make demands.*
> *Rule the kingdom and its lands.*
> *Power!*
>
> *Come on, brothers, side by side,*
> *In an army long and wide.*
> *Let nothing you and me divide.*
> *Power!*

"Power," Gully shouted again.

"Not so loud," Sammy told him. "We don't want Skink's mom to shut us down."

"Brothers side by side," the golem said, holding out his fist. He waited until the others bumped his fist with theirs. Then he smiled grayly.

"I'm not so sure about that last line." Skink looked at Sammy, "And, Dude, your cousin really doesn't look healthy. Like maybe he should be in the bed, not me."

"In the bed," Gully said, and sat down on the end with Sammy. The bed creaked ominously with his weight. "I'm all right, Dude."

"All right, all right," Skink said, moving a pen and the algebra paper to his lap. "Let's get this done so we can concentrate on music tomorrow night."

"Tomorrow night," Gully said. And a moment later, "I need a drum kit."

After that the two boys tackled their algebra homework. Gully listened carefully but added nothing to the conversation.

*Which*—Sammy thought—*is just as well since algebra terms wouldn't make a whole lot of sense without the algebra.*

That night, Sammy was too worried to fall asleep easily. He'd convinced his mother to let Gully stay overnight. His first overnight friend since they'd moved. *And*, he thought, *the friend turns out to be a hulking presence in the guest bed, neither sleeping nor breathing. Just there. Just like in a monster movie.* Then giggling silently, he whispered to himself, "It's alive! Alive!"

When he finally fell asleep, Sammy's dreams were wild, filled with vivid images of James Lee, Gully, Julia Nathanson, Reb Chaim, his parents. Each successive dream was worse than the one before as he was hurt, humiliated, punched, punished, and preached at.

He awoke sweating and miserable. The sun was barely up and he could hear the morning paper—*Dad must be the last person on earth to* not *get his news from the Internet*—just hitting the front porch.

Sammy turned over in bed to look at the mound that was Gully.

He wasn't there!

"Oh, no!" Sammy gasped.

He stumbled downstairs, feeling far older than his not quite thirteen years. But Gully wasn't downstairs either, and the front door was wide open.

Racing around the house, Sammy looked in the living room, dining room, kitchen—every room but his parents'. Then, thinking maybe Gully had decided to return to his origins or to make a girl golem of his own, Sammy checked his dad's workshop as well.

No Gully.

Fearfully, he went out to the porch to collect the paper, expecting to see Gully sitting in the swing or on the porch stairs. After all, the door had been open.

No Gully.

Sammy brought the newspaper inside, spreading it out at the kitchen table. He began turning through the pages to see if there was any word of a large, shambling gray, nonbreathing figure roaming the streets of their little town.

No Gully.

Then, just to be sure, Sammy clicked on the tiny kitchen TV his mom had gotten before they moved to the new house. He found the early-morning breaking news, something he never watched. War, drought, economic collapse. The Czech Republic was even mentioned.

*How strange is that!*

Then the local news began. A stolen bicycle, a high

school student caught tagging, someone's cat killed in a hit-and-run accident. And Mr. Grambling's music store broken into.

Suddenly alert, Sammy listened carefully. *Someone had smashed in the front door and walked out with . . .*

"Oh, no!"

*. . . a drum kit.*

The newscaster went on to mention the smashed door again, saying how it seemed to have been destroyed by someone with superhuman strength. He liked that phrase so much, he turned to the woman newscaster next to him and said it again. "Superhuman strength."

"Yes," she agreed, "and the police could find no discernible fingerprints anywhere."

"That's because I didn't give him any," Sammy said to the TV. He put his head in his hands, thinking that nothing could get any worse.

Just then he heard the unmistakable sound of drums coming from the basement. Nothing just became worse!

"Why didn't I check there first?"

Sammy ran to the basement stairs, afraid of what he might see. Stepping down three steps, he bent over to peek. Gully was sitting behind a simple drum kit: two cymbals, two toms, bass, snare, and high hat, hammering away.

Smash!

Crash!

*Actually*, Sammy thought, stunned, *he's not bad*. As he listened to the steady beat, all thought of where the kit had come from fled and his head bounced up and down to the rhythm.

Gully looked up, as if preternaturally he'd realized someone was watching.

*Preternaturally's a* great *word*, Sammy thought. *Abnormal, miraculous, superhuman.* He suddenly remembered the anchorman saying "superhuman strength" and shuddered.

Spotting Sammy on the stairs. Gully did a quick snare-snare, crash and bass, as if accenting the joke.

"Not a big drum kit," he said. "Room for four of us."

Sammy thought: *It* is *the perfect size kit not just for the space, but for the kind of band we're going to be.* And then he thought: *And what kind of band is that? Klezmer/Jazz/Pop/ Rock Fusion!* With a mythical creature on a stolen drum kit, a wounded martial artist on guitar, a terrifically smart girl on the fiddle, and a Jewish punching bag on the clarinet. He began to laugh wryly to himself. Actually—it was *everything* he'd ever wanted.

*And maybe* . . . he thought of Julia as he'd last seen her, dark hair bouncing as she walked away with her lunch tray . . . *maybe something more.*

"Hey," his father shouted from the kitchen. "What's that unholy racket?"

*Unholy.* Sammy suddenly remembered Reb Chaim's warning. *Oh, Dad—if you only knew.*

But Gully hadn't hurt anyone who hadn't deserved it. And Sammy was quickly getting used to not being kicked around. To having some power.

*People who listen to dire warnings—however well meaningly they are offered—*he decided, *NEVER get the power.*

The old saying about "red skies in the morning, sailors take warning" popped into his head and he thought of a better last line to Skink's song:

> *Come on brothers, side by side,*
> *In an army long and wide.*
> *We won't wait for time nor tide,*
> *Power!*

For the first time in what Sammy believed was ever, school was great. With Gully at his side, he didn't see James Lee or his Boyz all day. Julia Nathanson sat with him at lunch again. He wasn't *quite* as nervous this time, and actually managed to have a little conversation with her before the bell rang. And he didn't spill anything on himself in the process. In the lunch table conversation, they'd arranged for practice that evening. Which meant Julia was coming over to his house.

*Tonight!*

His stomach felt weird. He was surprised he kept the lunch down.

Sammy and Gully rushed home from the bus stop and headed right to the basement.

"C'mon, Gully, we've got to get the music area ready."

Gully grunted in response.

Under Sammy's direction, Gully moved shelves, chairs, and the drum kit around for forty-five minutes, until everything was in almost the same exact spot it had started in.

"There," Sammy said, "that looks good." Gully snorted but didn't say anything. Not even an echo: "That looks good!"

At dinner, Sammy's parents were very supportive of him having practice but . . .

"You have to finish your homework first," his mother said. She didn't look at Gully who was staring at his plate without eating, having spent fifteen minutes simply pushing the noodles around from one side of the plate to the other. "And Gully probably has homework, too. You can do it downstairs in the band room."

*Band room!* Sammy grinned.

He gulped down his pasta and then took the stairs

to the basement three at a time with Gully right behind. Homework was done quickly, though probably not well. Gully sat the whole while at the drum kit, making the motions but not the sound, his gray face full of concentration which made him look, Sammy thought, a bit like a sentient mushroom.

Afterward, they went upstairs to Sammy's bathroom, where Sammy washed up and changed into fresh clothes while Gully stared at himself in the mirror.

"I have homework, too?" Gully said to the mirror.

"Don't be silly," Sammy told him. "I've already done it for you. Your real homework—and schoolwork—is me."

They went back down to the band room. Gully riffed a bit on the drums while Sammy assembled his clarinet. Just as it was done, the doorbell rang. The sudden sound was as loud as an alarm.

It had all happened too fast for Sammy and once again his stomach lurched.

"Skinner John's here, Sammy," his mother called. "And a girl, too."

"Julia," said Gully. "Julia is a girl."

Sammy gulped, put down the clarinet, picked it up again. "Get a hold of yourself, Samson," he said sharply.

"Yeah," Gully echoed, "get a hold of yourself, Samson."

Shaking his head, Sammy stood with little grace and a lot of knee-knocking, and went upstairs to get the door, the clarinet in his hand.

*How did I ever think this was going to work?*

Gully trailed right behind repeating, "Get a hold. Get a hold."

At his last school, Sammy had done a butterfly project for science. It felt like every single one he'd ever studied had taken up residence in his belly. *There must be a million monarchs and red admirals and painted ladies in there.*

Skink was standing in the hallway, holding his guitar case. Julia was next to him, her violin case sporting a shiny fish symbol on which the word *gefilte* was emblazoned. Skink still looked pretty beat up, but he was walking without a cane, albeit stiffly.

"Gully, help him," Sammy said, and Gully carried Skink's guitar down the stairs.

At the same time, Sammy reached for Julia's fiddle. She just looked at him as if he were crazy and pushed past him to follow Gully down to the band room.

*Oh God*, Sammy thought. *Why would I think she*

*needed help carrying a fiddle that probably weighs, at most, two pounds?*

Skink stopped in front of him, giggling. "You're like, a true gentleman, Samson." Then he, too, went down into the basement, though slowly, holding tight to the railing and stopping on every other step, like a survivor from the *Titanic*.

Sammy remained at the top of the stairs as if someone had stapled his shoes to the floor, his hand absurdly out as if still waiting to grab Julia's violin case. *Well, this night couldn't have started much worse*, he thought. *But at least it's got nowhere to go but up.*

Suddenly his feet could move again, and he stomped down into the basement.

But it *did* get worse. As soon as everyone finished tuning—no mean feat, with Gully continually pounding on the drums—they all went quiet and stared at Sammy.

He didn't notice. Still mortified by his performance upstairs, Sammy was staring at the top of his shoes. It wasn't until the silence stretched out into total discomfort that he looked up to see everyone looking to him for direction.

*Why me?* he thought. *It's my first band, too!*

He looked back down at his shoes intently as if there were instructions printed on them and waited for someone else to speak.

Skink plucked a single note, then adjusted his tuning a micrometer.

Julia tightened her bowstring.

Gully startled them all by hitting a cymbal with a terrible crashing sound.

*Okay, Samson. Your basement, your band. Get this thing rolling or call it quits.*

"Skink," he said, his voice cracking. "Er . . . how about that song you wrote in the hospital. I've got a new last line for you."

Skink nodded. "I worked the chords out," he said, fingering a chord experimentally. "I think."

Sammy smiled at him. "Let's call it a *grober* and see who gives it a *frassk*."

"What in the world does *that* mean?" Skink asked.

"I have no idea," Sammy admitted. "It was something my grandfather used to say."

"My grandfather used to say, 'Let's kill it and see who sits *shiva*,'" Julia said.

"Oh." Skink chuckled. "My father says, 'Let's run it up the flagpole and see who salutes.'"

Gully was silent for a moment, then said, "My father said, '*Shalom aleichem.*'"

The three stared at him, then Julia smiled. "*Aleichem shalom.*"

After that, Skink strummed the first chord of "Power" and began singing.

After the first verse, Sammy figured out the key and began playing a low bass line on the clarinet. Almost immediately, Julia came in with a high descant on the violin. Surprisingly, Gully played the drums with skill, if way too loud; at times they could barely hear Skink singing.

*We'll need a PA system. For the vocals*, Sammy thought.

But even with the drums too loud and the guitar too soft and Julia's harmony on the chorus all but inaudible, Sammy knew they had something. He'd been playing music for nearly his whole life, and he could tell.

*I don't know what it is*, he thought. *It's going to need a lot of work. And it might be a long time before we're ready to leave the basement and play a gig. But we definitely have Something.* Then he stopped thinking and just blew . . .

After a half hour on Skink's "Power" song, Sammy taught them all the Rabbi Chaim song:

*Going down the road*
*In the Bar Mitzvah bus,*
*Boogie and klezmer*
*And fusion 'R' Us.*
*Making some music*
*And making a fuss.*

And then Julia said, a bit shyly—*not her usual style at all*, Sammy thought—"I wrote something, too. I was going to wait a bit before playing it. And I only have a first verse. It's called "Shiva." I wrote it when my grandfather Velvul died."

"Velvul," Gully said.

"It means Wolf," Julia explained. "In the old country."

"The old country," Gully repeated. "Czech Republic."

"Actually," Julia said, "it was the Ukraine."

Gully nodded. "The Ukraine." But his face looked even more blank than usual.

Julia didn't respond to that, but instead began playing one of the sweetest tunes Sammy had ever heard, her eyes closed as if to keep tears from falling. She got through the first verse, stopped, opened her eyes, and said, "In case you don't know, shiva is the week of mourning for Jews. We light a *Yahrzeit* candle on the anniversary of the death. A Year Candle." Then she began to sing again from the beginning, playing the fiddle at the same time:

> *It's been a year, Papa, your candle glows.*
> *And where you've gone to no one knows.*
> *The candle flame blows high and higher,*
> *I see your dear face in the fire.*
> *You are my first death. Now you're gone.*
> *We do not forget, but life goes on.*
>
> *Life goes on, I'm not sure why,*
> *Just watch me Papa, from on high.*
> *Life goes on, for me not you,*
> *I'm singing now, full klezmer blue.*

She almost yodeled the last note. It was klezmer crossed with the blues crossed with a kind of throaty sob that spiraled down even as her fiddle sang higher and higher until it almost hit a note that only dogs could hear.

Sammy was stunned. *I play music*, he thought. *So does Skink. But Julia's a musician!* The strange thing was, he wasn't jealous, just awestruck. *Completely and totally and till the end of time, awestruck*, he told himself.

"Life," Gully said solemnly. "Life goes on."

Sammy gulped. For the very first time, he wondered what kind of life Gully really had?

And then he thought: *Probably better than being a teapot or a bowl.* But he wasn't sure he entirely believed that.

"Kids," Sammy's mother called down the stairs. "It's after nine and you all have school tomorrow."

So the first practice was over as quickly as that. Julia loosened her bow. Sammy disassembled his clarinet. Skink latched his case shut over his guitar. Gully tucked his drumsticks into a pouch that hung from the snare.

"Tomorrow night?" Julia asked. It was barely a question. She was back to her old self and no longer sounded shy.

"Like, yeah!" Skink said, and held his fist out. Everyone bumped it, even Gully who had to stand and lean out over the drums.

## 18

*Practice Makes . . .*

"Julia's getting a glass of water and her mom is on her way," Sammy's mother said, "and I'll run Skinner John home. Your dad is working in his studio so don't bother him, Sammy. Oh—and does Gully need a ride?"

"Um . . . can he stay over again?" Sammy asked, suddenly frantic, thinking quickly, *What do I do if Mom says no? Where will Gully go then?*

His mother shook her head, and Sammy's thoughts raced on. *What if Gully breaks into another store? Or what if he goes after James Lee again?*

"It's a school night, Sammy," his mother said, and that was that. *It's a school night* was mom-speak for "Speak no more. Brush teeth. Get in bed."

"Okay." *Only it's far from okay*, he thought. "He doesn't need a ride."

Sammy's mother nodded as she shooed Skink out the front door. Then she turned and waved at the other kids. "Good night, Julia. Night, Gully."

"Good night, Mrs. Greenburg," Julia said, and Gully echoed her a half dozen octaves lower in his booming voice. "Good night, Mrs. Greenburg."

As soon as his mother was gone, Sammy pushed Gully out the door, and then they both watched from the front step as the car drove off.

"Gully," Sammy whispered, "stay close. Stay out of sight. And meet me at school tomorrow morning. Think you've got it? That's three things."

"Stay close. Out of sight. School tomorrow." Gully smiled. "Got it." He walked into the darkness.

Sighing, Sammy called after him. "And don't steal anything more!"

"Anything more," came Gully's echo back.

Sammy didn't know if that meant Gully understood, or if he let off the *don't steal* part on purpose. Either way, it didn't make Sammy comfortable. He thought about running after Gully but just then Julia came out to the porch with a glass of water in her hand. Sammy suddenly realized they were alone. His father was in his workshop and wouldn't have noticed a bomb falling on the house.

Sammy waited a moment for his stomach to do flips. But it felt . . . okay. Well, maybe not okay, but not as if he was going to throw up in front of Julia, a vast improvement from earlier in the evening.

"Good practice, Sammy," she said. "I think we've really got something."

"I was thinking exactly the same thing earlier."

Julia cocked her head to one side and smiled at him. "Really?"

*Whoops, there goes my stomach.* "Um . . . yeah."

"Did you like my song?"

*Loved it.* "Um . . . yeah."

Julia frowned and Sammy's stomach dropped through his shoes.

"Oh," she said.

Apparently, "um . . . yeah" wasn't ringing praise.

*C'mon Sammy! Where's that astounding vocabulary of yours?* Sammy thought. *Astounding. That's a good word. And the perfect one, as well.*

"I thought it was . . . astounding," he managed.

Julia's lips turned ever-so-slightly upward.

"Amazing."

She cocked her head again.

"Astonishing," he said, and she broke into an outright grin.

"Thanks, Sammy," she said. "Three A's! That's A-OK. I think the song's pretty good, too." She scrunched her eyes up a little. "Needs some more verses, though. But you've got a real way with words. Think you could work on it some?"

"Sure." Sammy grinned. He gathered his courage. "We'll work on it together. I'll see if I can come up with something for tomorrow. For . . . for us to work on." Saying *us* out loud made his stomach do flip-flops. *Out go the butterflies, in come the acrobats.*

Headlights flashed before she could answer.

"There's my mom," she said, handing Sammy her empty glass.

*How can she be so cool about this?* Sammy thought, standing with the glass pressed against his chest. He could feel the warmth where Julia's fingers had touched it. *Did she even notice the* us, *and the* together *parts?*

But Julia showed no sign of noticing his distress nor seemed to entertain any of her own. Going back inside the house, she scooped up her violin, then scampered out and down the drive. As she opened the car door to get in, Julia called back to him, "Yeah, we'll work on it together." Then she hopped in the car and rode away.

Sammy waved after them. The glass of water was still eerily warm in his hand.

The telephone's loud ring shattered the mood, and Sammy almost dropped the glass. No one . . . *no one* . . . ever called the house at that time of night. He went into the kitchen to pick it up, but his father was there before him.

"Yes, Rabbi," his father was saying. "Right now? But Sammy needs his beauty sleep before school . . . All right." He hung up and turned, saw the drawn look of horror on Sammy's face.

"Reb Chaim?" asked Sammy, all the while thinking, *Like I know any other rabbi up close and personal.*

"Yes. He wants to come over to talk with you. Now. And it's after nine on a school night, Samson. Is this about . . ."

"We'll be fast, Dad. I promise. Just bar mitzvah stuff, I'm sure." The lie felt like glue on his tongue.

Before his mother returned from taking Skink home, Sammy saw low-slung headlights and the rabbi pulled up in front of the house in a battered old Mustang.

Thinking it best to speak with Reb Chaim without the intervention of his father, Sammy ran outside.

The rabbi rolled down the window. "I want to know if it's done." Sammy wondered that the rabbi hadn't even started with "Shalom" or "Hello," or even a "Sorry to be doing this so late at night."

"Not yet," Sammy said, his voice breaking between the two short words. "I didn't think tonight . . ."

"That's the problem, Samson. You didn't think before and so you have to think *now*. Where is that creature?"

"Gully?"

"Who else?"

"I don't know where he is." *And that*, thought Sammy, *is the truth*.

The rabbi got out of the car and, though he wasn't much taller than Sammy, he seemed to tower over him. He put a hand on Sammy's shoulder. It felt like a lead weight. "Then find out, Samson. Before someone, *anyone*, gets hurt."

Sammy opened and shut his mouth several times, then said, "He's not a creature. He's a . . ."

"A what?"

"A . . . drummer," Sammy said. "The drummer in my band. And you know, Rabbi, he's pretty good, too."

"So you have a mindless monster in your band, beating on things, and you think that's good?"

"How is that bad?" asked Sammy, wanting to shrug off the rabbi's hand and not daring to. "My parents like him. My friends like him . . ."

"Have you not listened to a thing I've said?"

Sammy drew in a deep breath. "I think you're wrong, Rabbi." He wondered if that sentence had ever been spoken in all of history.

Reb Chaim withdrew his hand. "I am often wrong about things, my boy, but not about this." He seemed to stand a little taller, showing a bit of military bearing. "I studied golems. I made golems. I trained golems. I probably know more about golems than anyone living." He stared hard at Sammy. "You cannot reason with them. You must destroy them. And destroying them was the second-hardest thing I've ever done."

Sammy didn't want to ask but knew it was expected of him. "What was the hardest?"

"Burying all my friends in the desert." Reb Chaim turned abruptly and got back in his car. "I will give you another few days, but the creature must be disposed of. And that's that. No one else can do it for you—not me, not the police. Not the army. Not your parents. Not your friends. Only you, Samson. Only you. If they try, they can . . . no, they *will* be seriously hurt. And it will be *your* fault and *your* guilt and *your* enduring sorrow. Trust me on this."

"He's a *good* drummer," Sammy started to say as the car began to move away. It was then he saw a dark shadow running swiftly toward them.

The car started up and for a moment it looked as if the golem and the Mustang were about to collide.

"No, Gully," Sammy shouted, running toward the shadow and waving his arms. "He's a *good* one."

The shadow skidded to a stop, and a small voice came threading across the grassy verge. "On . . . the . . . right."

"Come here, Gully." Sammy put as much authority in his voice as he could.

The shadow came forward, dropping something dark behind, as if a bit of the shadow had detached from his hand.

"Why are you hanging around the house? What if Mom and Dad see you?"

Gully hung his head and mumbled something. It sounded like *My first breath*.

Sammy couldn't be sure. He wondered if Gully had begun to actually breathe. "You need to hide, big guy.

Maybe down by the river. Just be careful. Don't get caught. Keep breathing."

"Be careful." Gully grinned, and in the dark, with just the house light on him, his teeth were even grayer than before. "Keep breathing."

"Go," Sammy said. "Go."

"Don't get caught," Gully said as he walked off into the dark.

Sammy turned, went inside the house without looking back. But the breath thing was nagging him. What *had* Gully meant by "my first breath"? Was he becoming more and more human as the days went on. *Because*, Sammy thought, *if that's true then I can't kill him. It would be . . . wrong.*

Only as he walked into the kitchen to get a glass of water for his nightstand did Sammy finally realize what Gully had really said. Gully never invented anything new, just repeated things, though in interesting and surprising ways. But Sammy knew with a sudden chill that Gully had not said *breath*. He'd simply repeated a line from Julia's song: "My first death."

It was a chilling thought. He'd no idea what death meant to Gully.

For a brief moment he thought about getting a

flashlight and going outside to find the piece of shadow that Gully had dropped. Then he shook his head. Nothing on earth was going to take him outside again. Not tonight.

"Did you talk to the rabbi?" his father called from the studio.

"Everything's fine, Dad," Sammy called back. But of course everything wasn't.

*It might never be fine again.*

## 19

*The Principle of the Thing*

In the morning, after a night of horrible dreams in which a phalanx of gray goblins marched in and out of his house, Sammy got dressed quickly and went outside. The dawn sky was pearly, the street empty of cars. He stood at the edge of the driveway, desperately telling himself that he didn't have to walk out to where the golem had dropped a shadow from its shadow hand.

*But I have to know.*

With a sigh, he stepped off the pavement and began kicking through the high grass. Moments later, his sneakers starting to soak through with dew, he found what he hoped he wouldn't: a coyote's bedraggled tail— minus the coyote body.

Sammy stared down at it, wordless for once. The

gray and white fur was flecked with red, the stump end covered with flies. It stank. A few feet away, he noticed the coyote's head, crushed, its teeth set in a horrible grimace and a single eye staring out of a nest of bone shards.

There wasn't a body anywhere close by. He didn't look any farther for it.

Turning back, he shuddered and it felt as if worms were tunneling through his entire body.

But, he told himself, Gully isn't fast enough to catch a coyote.

Though to be honest, the golem could move quickly.

But a coyote? Even a dog might have trouble doing that.

Sammy got to the porch, looked over his shoulder at the tract of land that sloped down to the little river, and shuddered again.

Was the coyote coming after me? He'd never heard of a coyote doing that. Unless . . . unless it had been rabid. That was a small comfort. But the truth was, he didn't actually know for sure if Gully had caught and crushed the coyote or a car or truck or bus had. And if something else had, why did Gully pick up the carcass, and carry it around like . . . like a talisman. He liked the word talisman which was a kind a magical amulet. Maybe Gully had been hauling the awful thing around as a child would a blankie. That made Sammy giggle uncomfortably.

But then he thought: What matters is that Gully called it "my first death."

Sammy tried to remember whether the golem had emphasized the word first. And if he had, was he planning a second? Sammy couldn't bring up the actual whisper from his memory; it was all shades and shadows now. Shadows and shades.

The next two weeks Sammy felt as if he were two people, one safe and happy, the other fearful and watching. Some of the time watching out for the Boyz, part of the time watching out for another visit from Reb Chaim, and all of the time watching out for Gully.

The four band members met in school, exchanged ideas about songs in the hallway, did their homework in study hall together, tried out new verses at lunchtime, before assembling after dinner for band practice at Sammy's.

At those times Sammy thought—no, he *knew*—that

he'd never been happier. He had three actual friends who were as smart as he was. *Well, maybe smarter,* he thought generously. Then considering Gully, amended that. *Some who are smarter than I am.* He had a best friend, a girlfriend. *Well, a friend who's a girl,* anyway.

And a protector.

Best of all, they had a band.

In the early days, they simply played the four songs they'd already written—"Speaking with Chaim," had turned out to be a rocking success, with a kicking solo for Skink. "To Life!" gave Sammy a place to really shine on the clarinet. And when they got to "Shiva," Julia's fiddle sang so sweetly, Sammy had to blink quickly so as not to cry each time they played it. Especially when she told him how much she loved the verse he'd added.

As for Gully, he kept a good beat. Nothing fancy. But solid. Except on "Power!" and then he really let go, banging on the drums with such abandon, Sammy was afraid he'd break them and have to go back to the music store to steal another kit.

Those were the good times. But when he was alone or in bed or having to lie to his parents about why once again he wasn't going to bar mitzvah class, the words

"Two wrongs . . ." kept running through his head. Not for a song, but as a warning. He could almost hear Reb Chaim saying, "Finish him off. And do it soon." Then the shivering would start again, the coyote's broken head figuring in his dreams.

Almost hourly when he was awake, Sammy had arguments with himself: *Gully's not bad. He's a band member. A friend. A protector.* He'd sigh aloud, theatrically, still making the counterarguments to the rabbi in his head. *Isn't a coyote—maybe a* rabid *coyote—small payment for that?*

Sometimes his answer was no. But more and more often, it was yes.

After the two weeks of band practice, Sammy's parents surprised him with a present: a small PA system made up of two speakers, three microphones with stands, a four-channel mixing board, and enough cords to run among them all—if the cords didn't get all tangled up when Gully "helped" set the PA up. It was nothing big, but plenty loud enough to let them hear their vocals over the drums.

"You've been working so hard," Sammy's mother said, "we thought we'd help. Skink's parents and Julia's chipped in, too. I tried to find Gully's family, but they're not in the phone book or online."

"They . . . they don't speak English and are living on . . . on . . ." he couldn't think of the word. "On very little," he said. "They had to stretch to get the drum kit and . . ." And then he ran out of invention.

"Well, we won't say a word," his mother assured him.

"I can't wait to tell the others. About the PA system, I mean," Sammy said, hauling the conversation off Gully's family and back on track.

His father tried to look stern, but the obvious joy the gift had given Sammy was causing a smile to creep onto his face. "And as long as your schoolwork doesn't suffer, you can practice all you like." He gave up trying to frown and grinned fully. "And we get backstage passes to your first gig!"

*A gig!* Sammy bit his lip. Were they even close to being ready? But then he grinned. "You remember what Gram used to say?"

His parents said together, "From your lips to God's ears!"

And at the moment of saying it, Sammy got an idea for yet another song for the band.

✷

Along the way, the band wrote two other songs. One was "God's Ears" and the other was called "Bar Mitzvah," that Sammy began this way:

> *Today I am a man, I am a man today.*
> *I think of many manly things, I have no time to play.*
> *My voice is very deep, my thoughts are quite deep, too.*
> *I am a man today. I have no time for you.*

Skink started the next verse with a single line:

> *I've put down childish things, I've taken up the sword.*

Then he kind of backed away from it. "Er, the 'childish thing' line comes from the New Testament, not the Jewish Bible. One of my dad's favorite lines. I could, like, take it out . . ."

"No, no, it's great!" Sammy said. "We're not a Jewish band after all. We do klez, we do jazz, and rock and pop and soul and . . ."

The others agreed.

"It's GREAT!" Gully's drumsticks crashed onto the cymbals. As always, his enthusiasm was over the top.

Then Sammy came up with:

*I skewer with a phrase, I pinion with a word.*

"I like that," Julia said. "Especially pinion."

"What does that, like, mean?"

Julia leaned forward. "Shackle."

At the same time, Sammy said, "Tie someone's arms."

Then they laughed and sorted out the meanings.

Gully thought a minute.

*Today I am a man; I have two feet of clay.*

This startled Sammy for two reasons. First, he'd never heard Gully say anything he hadn't already heard. And second, it was so . . . so . . . darn appropriate!

Then, almost as if in a waking dream, Sammy realized that he *had* said just that phrase—"feet of clay"—sang it actually, when he'd been feverish, and making the golem. He couldn't remember if this had been before or after he fashioned the head, before or after he put in the ears. Maybe the clay itself had heard and remembered. He started to giggle out loud.

"Well, *I* think it's a grand line," Julia admonished, then winked over at Gully who actually blushed a slight grayish red.

"A grand line," Gully replied.

"A *very* grand line," Sammy said quickly. "Great going, Gully."

Gully did a quick taradiddle on the drums and said over and over again, "Great going, Gully! Great going, Gully," grinning all the while.

Sammy thought suddenly, *If Reb Chaim could see how good and fun Gully can be, he wouldn't* . . . but then he let the rest of that thought dribble away. He didn't think any such argument would convince the rabbi.

Skink said, "But we, like, need a last line to the verse."

For a moment, they all were solemn, thinking. Then Sammy repeated the three lines:

*I've put down childish things; I've taken up the sword.*
*I skewer with a phrase; I pinion with a word.*
*Today I am a man; I have two feet of clay.*

"Feet of clay," Gully shouted, raising one drumstick, and then added, "Power!"

"Wait a minute . . . wait a minute," Skink said, his pointer fingers making circles around each other, "how about repeating the line: *I think of manly things; I have no time to play.*"

Julia shook her head. "Too easy. Too slick. Too . . ."

"Not if we tweak it a bit," Sammy said.

"Tweak it a bit," Gully parroted. "I am a man, I . . ."

"No!" Sammy stood up. "I am a grown-up now, I have no time to play."

*Ta-boom!* went the big drum. *Crash!* went the cymbal. Gully grinned so hard, all his gray teeth showed.

"All we need now is a chorus," Sammy told them.

"Tomorrow." His mother's voice sang down the stairs. "You can work on the chorus tomorrow. Time to go home, kids. Julia your mom is here. Skink, your dad's on the way. Gully . . ."

"Time to go home," Gully shouted up at her. "I am a man."

*Gully's home?* Sammy still didn't know where the golem spent his nights. *Maybe down by the little Mill River at the bottom of the meadow, murmuring clay thoughts to the mud in the riverbank. Murdering small animals.* He stopped the thoughts from running on. He didn't want to ask. He didn't want to know.

More weeks passed idyllically, and Sammy thought his life couldn't be more perfect. Like living in the garden of Eden *actually*—but there was always going to be some snakes. He didn't want to think about that.

Gully had become part of the scenery at school and at home. Sammy couldn't even remember the last time he'd worried about it being discovered the golem wasn't Amish or Czech or his cousin. They were in many classes together, and Sammy had to do Gully's homework as well as his own, but it was a small price to pay for peace.

His parents had stopped questioning him about Hebrew school. He told them the rabbi was sick, or moving away. It turned out they hadn't been all that set on his bar mitzvah after all. His dad said he could use the extra time on the wheel, not driving all that way. They liked the band.

Skink was all healed, and his guitar playing seemed to have leaped several paces forward, probably in response to Julia's fiddle. The surprise was that he was especially good at klezmer, which his mother laughingly said, "Because I was pregnant with him when we were in Israel!"

"Who knew," Skink said. "Maybe I should have that bar mitzvah instead of you, Word Man."

The band's table at lunch—they called it the Tour-Bus-Your-Own-Table—was so much in demand by the seventh and eighth graders that they had to establish a rolling alphabetical seating plan.

And Julia . . .

*Well, Julia is* . . . For the first time in his life, Sammy was totally at a loss for words.

In fact, everything was going so well, Sammy got a little careless.

*A little!* he was to think later, *is an understatement. And* I never *make understatements!* Which was an understatement of its own!

He'd sent Gully on ahead to sit at the Tour-Bus-Your-Own-Table, which was now just called the TBYOT, which sounded like Hebrew but wasn't. *Or at least*, Sammy thought, *I don't think it is.*

Sammy ducked into the bathroom. After all, James Lee and his crew had simply faded into the woodwork over the last few weeks, afraid of tackling Gully and forced to listen to Sammy and his friends *and* their hangers-on singing at the lunch table, showing off their new songs a cappella, which—as Sammy explained every time meant singing without instruments

And each time, Gully added, "And without caps"

which hadn't been funny the first time Sammy had cracked the joke. But everyone laughed. *Maybe*, Sammy thought, *it's the way Gully says it, with that strange, flat, gray voice.*

So carelessly, and without his bodyguard, Sammy walked into the boys' bathroom.

And almost walked right into James Lee.

"Well, well, well," James Lee said in a lazy voice. He looked Sammy up and down the way a large carnivore looks at a much, much smaller herbivore. "One little bug all alone. Just the bug . . . and the bug *swatter.*"

Without thinking, Sammy shot back, "Or the brain and the brain*less*." Realizing he'd probably said too much, he began to edge toward the door, then turned to run out. But James Lee was too quick for him, grabbing him by the neck of his shirt and yanking him back inside.

Looking hopelessly around for help, Sammy realized they were the only ones there. The bell had rung. Everyone else was at lunch.

"You'd better not—" Sammy began, hoping to soften whatever beating was about to happen. He turned around, which made his shirt twist about his neck painfully.

James Lee laughed. "Better not what?" He clenched

the fist of the hand that wasn't holding on to Sammy's shirt.

Sammy noted frantically that water was dripping from that hand. *At least he washed after going. Or at least I hope he did!* "Better not touch me," he said in a voice that aimed for bravado and fell into whine. "Touch me and Gully will kill you. And do a dance step on your dead head. A regular kick line."

James Lee sneered. "You think I'm afraid of Graybug, you stinking Greenbug?" He swung Sammy around so that his body was now between Sammy and the door. Only then did he let go of Sammy's shirt, though to Sammy, the twist at the neck seemed just as tight as before.

James Lee started toward him, so close now, Sammy could smell his breath.

*Surprisingly minty.* Without thinking, Sammy started to giggle.

"You think that's funny, Bug Boy?" James Lee had two fists up now.

*Now or never,* Sammy thought. He faked left and dodged right, trying to scoot by, though he might as well have just jumped into James Lee's arms.

James Lee pushed him against the wall next to the urinals and put his face right up to Sammy's.

"I've beat up bigger guys than your Gray Gully, Bug," James Lee said.

"*Beaten*," Sammy said automatically. His mouth kept going, though he was sure his heart had just stopped.

"And been beat up by them, too. He's big, but my dad's bigger."

That seemed an odd thing to say, but Sammy didn't have time to think about it further. James Lee had already cocked his fist back for a big delivery. Sammy knew without a shadow of a doubt that he wasn't going to survive that kind of punch line.

"Okay!" a deep voice said from behind James Lee. "That's gone on far enough."

James Lee's bulk blocked Sammy's view, so he couldn't see who it was. But he didn't have to look—he recognized the voice.

*This is the first time I've ever been glad to see* him!

And then Sammy's relief manifested—*manifested, what a good word*. Sammy said it out loud, spitting the word into James Lee's face, adding: "I guess it's just the principle of the thing, Jamison."

"What thing?" James Lee asked, clearly puzzled.

He'd obviously been too intent on his own threats to hear anything else and his face had lost its usual snarl as he tried to puzzle through this new idea. "What are you talking about, Greenbug?"

Not waiting for an answer, James Lee swung at Sammy's head. But suddenly, a large hand landed on his shoulder, and he was turned around to face Mr. Kraft. Sammy watched, stuck somewhere between horror and amusement, as James Lee's cocked hand, missing its initial target, still kept going forward, right toward the principal's nose.

The Head Cheese didn't wait to get them to the office before giving his judgment. On one of them, anyway. He walked between the two boys and frankly, Sammy was relieved that the principal's bulk separated them.

"You're suspended, Joliette," Mr. Kraft snarled as soon as they were in the hall. "And lucky for you that blow never actually landed or the police would have had to be called in as well. Maybe you never got the memo, but punching out the principal is a big no-no."

Even though he was still shaking with fear and its aftermath, Sammy grinned. Pure nastiness he'd never understand. But snarkiness—well, that was his home ground.

"I didn't actually punch you," James Lee muttered.

"As I said," Mr. Kraft repeated, "lucky for you."

Sammy was thinking: *That wasn't luck. Principal Kraft is bigger and faster than James Lee. He blocked that punch.* For the first time, Sammy really looked at the principal, noticing light scars around the big man's eyes, how crooked his nose was. *Maybe being an educator wasn't his first choice of a career.* He tried to envision Mr. Kraft in boxing shorts and failed.

Then remembering the word suspension, Sammy looked over at James Lee to see if he had anything like a thought on his tiny mind. *Maybe he's thinking: A few days off will be nice.*

But Mr. Kraft wasn't done. "In-house suspension for you, Mr. Joliette."

"Aw, sir," James Lee whined, "that's like jail."

Mr. Kraft nodded, agreeing. "Which is precisely where you're going to end up if you keep on this path."

"Whatever, old man," James Lee said. He suddenly wasn't whining anymore.

Mr. Kraft sighed. "Get yourself down to the office, Joliette. And maybe I won't call *your* old man."

James Lee didn't exactly march meekly away. He squared his shoulders and walked off down the hall as if he—and not the principal—had won the argument.

*But he sure doesn't have that usual spring in his step.*

"And you," Mr. Kraft said, rounding on Sammy, "what were you *thinking*?" He didn't give Sammy a chance to answer. "You can't bait the bear and not expect to get bit."

"I never started anything with him!" Sammy protested. "He's been after me since the day I got here."

"Don't think I haven't noticed. However, I expected more from you, Mr. Greenburg. You are exceptionally bright about a lot of things, but evidently not about Joliette and his followers. You can't just ignore him and let it go, can you? You always have to make some kind of smart-aleck comment."

Sammy couldn't argue with that.

Arms folded, the Big Cheese leaned against the locker and looked over Sammy's head for a moment before going on.

"Listen, Mr. Greenburg," he began, then looked down at Sammy. "I'm trying to help you here. Joliette and his kind are bad seeds. But bad seeds always go to ground right where they're planted. You're not going to be in high school forever. Or even in this town. You're a good kid." He reached out and tapped Sammy on the forehead with one finger. "*And* you've got a brain. Use it. Don't rile these boys up."

"That's not fair, sir."

"Of course it isn't fair. But it's not fair to Joliette either. He's never had a chance of making something of himself. *You* do."

"That's not what I meant," Sammy grumbled.

Mr. Kraft smiled, and it struck Sammy that it might have been the first time he'd ever seen the Head Cheese smile. It made him look years younger.

"I know, Sammy, I know. I'm a pretty smart guy myself. That's why I'm the principal. Now, enough of this. Tell me about this band I've been hearing about. Because I've got an idea . . . and my ideas are usually good ones."

"An idea, sir?" Sammy tried to look interested. It was better than looking panicked. Felt better, too.

"You answer my question first. And don't ask another question in return. I can have that conversation with my wife's grandfather."

"Sir?"

They started walking again down the hall.

"My wife's Jewish and her grandfather's very old-fashioned, always answering a question with a question." He grinned. "And you are too young and hip to be sounding like him even though you're Jewish."

Sammy was so stunned at this news about the principal's wife that he was momentarily silent. "Er, you know I'm Jewish, sir?"

"I'm the principal here, Sammy. I know *everything* about my kids. It's in my job description, right after hiring and firing teachers and signing off on lunch menus." He grinned.

Sammy's mind was a whir of all the impossible things he'd just learned, and then remembered that the principal had asked him a question. But he couldn't remember what. "Um, what was the question again, sir?"

"The band, Mr. Greenburg. The band."

"It doesn't have a name yet," Sammy said, glad to be back on safe ground. "But it's a klezmer/jazz/pop/rock fusion band. We've got about five original songs so far, and I'm teaching them some actual klezmer tunes as well. And . . ."

"Them?"

"Ah, Skink—I mean Skinner John Williams—on guitar. Julia Nathanson on fiddle. She's *incredible!* And my . . . er . . . cousin Gully on drums."

"Ah Gully—that big gray boy. Is that his actual name?"

"It's Gulliver," Sammy said, remembering back to

the conversation with Julia. *Best to keep the story straight.*
"A family name."

"Funny name for a Jewish boy," Mr. Kraft mused.

"His father teaches English literature in . . ."

"In the Czech Republic. Good to know. And I'm delighted he's in the band. Drums sounds about right for him. I'm glad there's something he can do. He looks so lost much of the time."

*Lost? Gully?* Sammy had a hard time thinking of Gully that way.

"As if he's in a time and place not of his own choosing," Mr. Kraft was saying.

*Oh, Mr. Kraft, if you only knew. . . .* For a moment— just a moment— Sammy considered confiding in the principal, but then the moment passed.

By now they were at the principal's outer office. James Lee was nowhere in sight. Probably in the small side room the kids all called the Cell. It wasn't barred or locked or anything, as far as Sammy knew, but it didn't have any windows. At least that was what the others said. It was for the hard cases. Like James Lee.

"Come into my office, Mr. Greenburg." It wasn't an invitation so much as a command.

They went in and Mr. Kraft sat down in the rolling

chair behind his big desk. *His big* imposing *desk*, Sammy thought, the word imposing making as much of an impression as the desk. *For a big, imposing man.*

Sammy sat in the straight-back chair on the other side.

"This is my idea. Tell me what you think." Again it wasn't any kind of actual invitation. Mr. Kraft leaned back in his chair, held his hands behind his head, and said, "If you and your bandmates can stay out of trouble until the last football game and dance. . . ."

Sammy leaned forward. "That's next week."

The principal sat up in his chair, his head thrust out like a turtle's. "I know when it is, Sammy. I make the schedule. Right after signing off on the lunch menu."

"Yes, sir."

"That means no bear-baiting. No dogfights. No sassing. No snark . . ."

"No?"

"None!" The principal grinned. "Then your band—which will have a name by then—will be the opening act for Armageddon, which has been hired to play for the all-school dance. You'll have a half hour."

"A gig for us?" Sammy heard his voice squeak. "Opening for . . . Armageddon?" *It was only the best-*

*known band in the area. Maybe in the state!* "Will they let us?"

"I don't just have the ideas around here, Sammy. I make the decisions as well. Of course they'll *let* you."

"O—okay." Sammy gulped hard.

"I suggest BUG," Mr. Kraft said.

"BUG?" Another squeak.

"For the band's name. Better to own it than fear it."

"BUG?" For a moment Sammy couldn't say a word. Not for a long moment. At last he ventured, "I'll have to ask the band." He wondered how many minutes the principal had been standing at the bathroom door listening before he'd stopped things.

*Long enough to hear James Lee call me Bug*, he decided.

And then that thought was swallowed up by the pure joy of being offered an actual gig. *A GIG!*

The principal nodded. "Now, Mr. Greenburg, time to get over to the Tour Bus table. Lunch awaits.."

"You know about the Tour Bus table?"

"It's my school, Sammy. I know about *everything*!"

And with that Sammy was dismissed.


Sammy practically sprinted to the cafeteria, the words *A gig! A gig! A gig!* looping through his head.

He hadn't even begun thinking about gigs. *We only have five songs so far. And some klezmer dance tunes, though we're still a bit wobbly on those. I thought we'd need more songs before . . .*

(A gig! A gig! A gig!)

*But it's an opening slot. Half hour. Five songs is plenty for that.*

(A gig! A gig! A gig!)

Crashing through the cafeteria's double doors, Sammy went right for Tour-Bus-Your-Own-Table, not even getting in line for food.

*First, good news*, he thought, *then bad food.*

"Guys," he said, "I've got great—"

He stopped. Erik Addison, the "smart" member of James Lee's Boyz—the one Sammy had shared detention with—was sitting at the table talking animatedly to Gully. The kids on the bench on the other side of the table were scrunched together because of the addition of Addison outside of the regular alphabetical rotation.

This is trouble.

Sammy glared pointedly at Skink, who shrugged. Julia had her face in her food, eating quickly because, as she liked to say, "I prefer to torture my taste buds for as little time as possible."

"Hey, Gully," Sammy said casually, "what's up?"

The golem glanced over and showed his gray teeth. He pointed to Erik. "Drums," he said. Which explained nothing.

But Erik grinned, looking almost shy.

If a leather-clad, shaved-head, behemoth could look shy, Sammy thought.

"Your cousin and I were talking about drums," Erik began. "I, um, play a little drums."

"He plays a little drums," Gully agreed.

*This can't get any weirder*, Sammy thought. But Erik didn't seem to be causing any trouble, and no one seemed to mind him sitting there . . . much. And I can't wait any longer to tell them about the gig!

"Guys," Sammy said, sitting down next to Julia, who nodded to him without pausing her ingestion of whatever mystery meat was being served today. "Guys, we have a gig."

"What?" and "Awesome!" Skink and Julia spoke so close together that Sammy wasn't sure which one said which. And Gully muddied the waters even further by saying, "What, awesome," just afterward. They grinned at each other and laughed, and even Erik said "Congratulations."

*He sounds genuinely pleased*, Sammy thought, which was weird, but no weirder than Sammy having a band and a gig and friends, and so Sammy was soon deep in discussion with his band about what they needed to do to get ready. All the other kids at the band table listened open-mouthed. None of them noticed when Erik left the table.

"We need another song," Sammy said at practice that night. They'd played their five songs, timing it with Skink's watch, and they'd come out to twenty minutes. "We need a seven- or eight-minute song to fill out the half hour."

"So not a little pop song," Julia said. "Something with meat. More of an anthem."

"Meat," Gully said, managing to sound hungry even though he never ate.

Skink picked a couple of thoughtful notes on his guitar. "Maybe something built around our band name. Like Bad Company's *Bad Company*." He looked up from his fret board. "And like, what is our band name, anyway?"

"Well," Sammy said, "Mr. Kraft thinks we should name ourselves BUG."

"What?" the band chorused the question together, almost as if it had been rehearsed.

"And I kind of agree with him." Sammy was as shocked as the others when these words popped out of his mouth.

"BUG? Why that?" Julia asked. "Isn't that what James Lee and his crew call you?"

"Better to own it, than fear it." Sammy didn't tell them that was what the principal had said.

Laughing, Skink did a run up and down the guitar. "I got it. Name it and shame it."

"Shame James Lee," added Gully. He hit the drumsticks simultaneously on the big cymbal. The crash was nearly deafening.

"Besides," Sammy said, enlarging on something he'd been thinking a lot about ever since his talk with Mr. Kraft, "the Beatles are named after bugs."

"Bugs are B-E-E-T-L-E-S," Julia said. "Not B-E-A-T-L-E-S."

"No—BUGS 'R' US," Sammy explained carefully. "And that's how we'll introduce ourselves. I'm Sammy GreenBUG. Gully is BUG—BIG UGLY GUY. Skink is BROWN ULTIMATE GUY. And Julia is . . ."

"Beautiful . . ." Skink said

"Unattainable . . ." Sammy added.

"Gurrrrrrrrl!" purred Julia.

"BUG!" Gully shouted.

Sammy thought about owning and naming and lines popped into his head. "I've got something," he said.

"Well, like, spill it!" Skink said, running a riff on his guitar.

Sammy began chanting:

> *You can fear it, or you can own it.*
> *You can dull it, or you can hone it.*
> *If you name it, then you shame it.*
> *BUG!*

Skink started chunking some thick chords behind the chant, and Julia doubled him on the low strings of her violin. Gully thumped the low tom of his kit in a vaguely Native American rhythm.

They thought a bit more and together came up with:

> *You can quit, or you can play.*
> *You can leave, or you can stay.*

*If you name it, then you shame it.*
*BUG!*

They all shouted the last word into their microphones, except for Gully, who didn't have one, but didn't really need one for his booming voice to be heard.

It was Skink who managed the next two lines.

*You can run, or you can fight.*
*You're not wrong if in the right.*
*If you name it, then you claim it.*
*BUG!*

"Then," Sammy said, "we stand up and claim it by each saying our BUG name. I could start. By saying, 'I'm Sammy GreenBUG.'"

"I'm Big Ugly Guy, Gully," said Gully.

"Brown Ultimate Guy." Skink played a quick series of chords underneath. "Skinner John Williams."

"And I . . ." Julia said, bowing up the strings and once again hitting that dog-calling high note, "am Beautiful Unattainable Girl." She blushed. "It sounds silly for me say it."

"She's—like—right." Skink nodded his head toward Julia. "It would be embarrassing for her."

"What if . . . *I* say it?" asked Sammy. "Will that help?"

Julia nodded, her cheeks now crimson.

"And then we repeat one of the verses," Sammy said to change the subject.

"No," Julia said, "we play the tune without words afterward, and when the last drumbeat crashes down, we all shout out 'BUG!' together, And lights out."

"Hey, that's like *very* cool," Skink said.

"Very cool!" Gully shouted.

"Very, very cool," Sammy said, very, very quietly, but everyone heard, especially Julia.

By then it was the end of practice. They could hear grown-ups laughing upstairs.

When the kids made their way into the kitchen, they found Julia's mother and Skink's mother had already arrived and were just finishing coffee with Sammy's parents. And when they told everyone about the gig, the adults sounded even more excited about it than the band had been.

"We'll definitely come," Mrs. Williams said to Skink, "your father and I."

Julia's mother promised an entire busload of relatives and neighbors, to which Julia rolled her eyes.

"Gully, will your mother be there?" Mrs. Williams asked.

Sammy threw his body into the way of that blast. "She works nights," he said.

Gully nodded. "Nights."

"Well," Sammy's mother said, "maybe she can get off work just this once. Or go in a little late."

"Gully will ask," Sammy said, "won't you, Gully?"

The gray teeth were set wide in a great gray grin. "I will ask."

And off he walked, out of the front door, into the dark, heading—Sammy was sure—down to the river to talk to the mud.

"He's a strange young man," said Julia's mother.

"He's Amish," Sammy's mother responded. "I'm not sure he understands everything we ask."

"I thought he was from the Czech Republic," Mrs. Williams mused.

Sammy got ready to panic as his conflicting lies were tossed out so casually, but both women merely shrugged and dropped the topic. Soon after, good nights were said, and everyone left.

"Sammy, can we talk?" his mother said as soon as the door was shut. "It's about Gully."

"Homework, Mom. It's already late."

She nodded. "Tomorrow will be fine."

He nodded. "Tomorrow." But all the while he was thinking: *Once more the BUG manages to escape the swatter!* Then he went down to the band room, took out his math homework, and played around with equations until one of them finally made sense.

Over the next week, Sammy escaped again and again. He was out the door early to school, and BUG practiced every night. He made sure there was no time to talk to his mother. Perhaps, seeing him so involved and happy with friends, she was willing to drop whatever concerns she'd had about Gully. Perhaps she realized Gully wasn't her business. Or perhaps she was just biding her time. As long as she didn't ask more questions, Sammy was content.

*Content*, he thought. *Or as much as an almost-thirteen-year-old can be.*

Besides, he was massively busy. Not only did he have daily homework. And papers. And tests. He had Gully's homework and papers, as well. He couldn't take any of

Gully's tests for him, of course. But Gully managed not to flunk them all.

And with the dance less than a week away, BUG had to run through their set list over and over, pretending they were actually at the gig. There were no stops, even if someone made a mistake.

"You can't stop in the middle of a song when you're playing live," Sammy reminded them.

Julia agreed. They were the only ones who'd actually ever played in front of people—and those were just a couple of recitals while they were both still playing classical music. Sammy wasn't sure those counted as gigs, but the rest of the band thought so.

And they didn't just practice the songs: they practiced the show as a whole. They made sure the transitions between the songs were smooth and not too long, that Sammy had some stage patter ready if Skink broke a string, or Julia had to tune her violin. Or if Gully . . . well, whatever Gully might do. Sammy shuddered thinking about that, then pushed it way to the back of his mind.

The phone rang Wednesday evening right before dinner. Sammy snagged the call. His parents were both too busy to pick up the phone.

His mother was wrestling with a leg-of-lamb roast, and losing.

And from the studio came the sound of his father singing at the potting wheel. Sammy knew that meant things were going so well that his dad would prefer a dish of food brought in rather than walking the twenty steps into the kitchen to eat with them. As he liked to say at such times, "The clay is a dictator, though a benevolent one."

"Got it!" Sammy yelled. When he saw who the call was from, he was hugely relieved he'd been the one to answer it.

"Er—hello, Reb Chaim," he said in a low tone, walking the phone out into the living room so neither of his parents could hear. "It's Sammy."

The rabbi didn't bother with a hello, but got right to the point. "The golem?"

"He's . . . doing well in school. And in the band, too," Sammy said. "He's our drummer."

"Of course he is," said the rabbi. "Until he isn't."

That was too opaque for Sammy. Unless the rabbi was talking about getting rid of Gully. Again.

"Really, you should come and hear him, Rabbi," Sammy said. "We've, ah, got a gig this weekend and I think you'll like him . . ."

"You should be having a gig with me every week, Samson," Reb Chaim said. "Learning Hebrew, preparing for your bar mitzvah. Instead you are playing with a fire that is going to burn down *your* house and everyone else's. I know this too well. As it is, I have given you too much time to do this thing and now I must demand you do it tonight. Now."

"Or what, Rabbi? You said yourself that only I could do it!"

There was silence on the phone for a moment. Then Chaim spoke softly. "I will think of something. Even if it kills me. Maybe then you'll see what it is that you've created."

"A friend, Rabbi," Sammy said. "I've created a friend and a musician for my band. We're pretty good, you know. It's a klezmer/jazz/pop/rock fusion band. We're called BUG, and we're opening for Armageddon at the high school this Saturday."

"*Armageddon!*" It didn't sound like a band the way the rabbi said it. "That's exactly what it will be."

Suddenly, the image of the dead coyote filled Sammy's mind, the snarling mouth, the staring eye. He almost dropped the phone. "What's that, Rabbi—Armageddon?"

"The end of the world, Samson. The end of *your* world."

Sammy took another big breath and whispered into the phone, "Hope you can make it, Rabbi." He didn't mean to sound snarky, but he did. Just a little.

"And I hope *you* can make it through to your concert, Samson," Reb Chaim said, with a little snark himself. "I will be there to help."

There was a click as the rabbi hung up.

Sammy wasn't sure what Reb Chaim had meant about being there to help. After all, Gully was all the help Sammy needed. And *he* was around all the time! And then he shuddered, because deep down he did know exactly what the rabbi meant.

"Who was that on the phone?" his mother called from the kitchen.

"Wrong number," Sammy said, the lie sour in his mouth, and heavy.

The kids at the Tour Bus table could talk about nothing but the upcoming gig. They even asked if they could— maybe one at a time—sit in on rehearsal.

"We'd be quiet," Bobby Marstall had promised, a finger to his lips.

But the band voted Bobby's request down that very night.

"I'm not ready to have someone sit in on rehearsal," said Julia. "I'm still making too many mistakes."

"None I noticed," Sammy said gallantly, though she'd actually just flubbed the high notes on her own song.

The next day, though, Sammy gave the Tour Bus table kids each a set list he'd printed up on his computer.

Even though he thought of it as a consolation prize, the list seemed to excite them even more.

"Wow," one girl said, "awesome titles."

The rest of the table agreed, arguing over what "Shiva" might mean, or "Power!"

Each time someone said "Power!" Gully reacted, slamming his big fist down on the table and growling the word. Soon the entire table of kids were doing it and looking pointedly over at James Lee's table.

Minus James Lee. He was once again in detention.

"He, like, owns the place," Skink said, nodding his head in the direction of the Boyz.

"The lunchroom?" Sammy asked, through a mouthful of mystery meat.

"No, detention."

Sammy couldn't help himself. He began to laugh, mystery meat spraying across the table.

Luckily Julia had already left.


The last rehearsal, they checked that the band's gear was ready and that they had spare strings and spare sticks, spare reeds and spare picks, and batteries.

"Let's rotate through," Sammy said. "Each of us check someone else's stuff."

It was Skink who suggested Julia bring her spare bow. Julia who asked Sammy to print up several extra set lists. And Sammy who made sure about the batteries, strings, picks, and extra reeds. Surprisingly, Gully himself found a second pair of drumsticks. Sammy didn't dare ask him where he'd gotten them. He was afraid he knew.

By dance weekend, everything about the show was polished and shiny, and still everyone was nervous when it finally arrived. The school had buzzed all Friday about the scheduled events, even the youngest kids, and about the dance that was to happen on Saturday night.

The football team, with James Lee finally back— though benched—had played their biggest rival on Saturday and won by a last-minute kick. The kicker had been Erik, the one who'd talked to Gully about drums. The team carried him on their shoulders, and everyone up in the wooden stands went wild, jumping up and down screaming and clapping and calling Erik's name, till the stands shook dangerously, and Mr. Kraft had to hold up his hands to quiet them. But he was grinning while he did it.

Only James Lee wasn't part of the celebration. Instead he sat fuming the whole time the school cheered.

"Look at him," Skink said, nudging Sammy with his elbow.

"Yeah, what a stoop," Sammy answered.

Julia agreed.

Sitting in front of the three of them in the stands, Gully started yelling, "Stoop, stoop, stoop!"

"Like—what's a *stoop*?" Skink asked.

"I assume it's short for someone stupid, someone who moans when a friend is celebrated," Julia said.

"Someone who wants all the glory," added Sammy.

Gully thought a minute.

*Or at least*—Sammy thought—*it looks like he's thinking. Only I never made him a brain.*

At last Gully spoke. "A stoop is someone who is like James Lee."

They all laughed. Even Gully.

That evening, when they met at Sammy's house to pack up the gear, it took only minutes before they started talking about how they felt.

"Butterflies," Julia said.

"Elephant in bowling shoes here." Sammy pointed to his forehead. A vein was throbbing. He was sure everyone could see it.

Skink said, "My fingers are itching, and not in a good way."

They turned as one to look at Gully who was standing seemingly unconcerned.

"Not hungry," he said at last.

For a moment, Sammy was startled. Then he remembered, it had been one of the very first things Gully had ever said. Quickly he added, "I'm not hungry, either. Must be the butterflies-in-stomach effect."

"We'll eat afterward," said Julia. "We'll be starving then!"

"The mics are packed," Sammy told them. "The rest of the PA is already in my dad's pottery van along with Gully's drums." He looked at Skink who was standing at the bottom of the basement stairs with his guitar in one hand an amp in the other. Gully and Julia were right behind him.

"Go! Go!" Sammy urged them. "Go on up. I'll get the lights."

And then they were gone.

He stood for a moment staring after their retreating backs, then turned. The basement looked strange to him, empty of all the gear that had filled it for the last few weeks. He only had to pick up his clarinet case and walk upstairs, out the door to the car. Still . . .

Skink had returned. "Hey, Samson, what's the hold up?"

Still staring at the room, Sammy muttered, "What am I forgetting?"

Skink cracked a sudden grin. "Like, shoes, Sammy."

Sammy blinked and stared down at his feet. "You're kidding!"

Julia suddenly poked her head down in the basement. "What's the hold up, fellas?"

Laughing, Skink said, "Sammy's deciding what shoes to wear."

Now Julia was looking at his feet, too, bare except for his socks. Sammy realized that just a week ago he would have died of embarrassment. But now he just laughed. "I'm thinking sneakers," he said, "but only because they're the only shoes I own."

That earned him a giggle from Julia that made his heart miss the next two beats.

"That's a shame," she quipped. "You'd look great in a pair of three-inch heels."

"Like—eeeeuuuuuw," Skink said, and headed back up the stairs.

"Channeling his inner girl," Julia quipped, following Skink back up.

"I'll meet you guys at the car," Sammy called after them before running up the stairs himself. "Don't want to be late to our first gig!"

Minutes later, he and Julia exchanged high fives, and then—all wearing shoes—they were off in the pottery van and the major's big car. The mothers had gone ahead to get good seats.

In the van, Sammy sat next to Gully wishing all the while he could have gone with Skink and Julia in the car. But of course he had to keep an eye on the golem.

*Sometimes it's hard to know who's protecting who.*

Maybe he needn't have worried. Gully wasn't talking and neither was his father.

Sammy giggled. Maybe we're all nervous.

"Something funny, Sammy?" his father asked.

"Just nerves."

Gully cleared his throat. "Butterflies," he said. "Elephant in bowling shoes here. My fingers are itching, and not in a good way."

"Oh, son, you've got it bad," Sammy's father said to Gully. "But don't worry, you guys will be terrific. I've heard some of your practice. Hard to miss it, actually. There's a lot of power in your little group."

Sammy knew what Gully was going to respond, but he wasn't quick enough to stop him.

"POWER!" Gully beat the extra drumsticks against the back of Sammy's seat.

"A little less volume, Gully," Sammy's dad said. "It's just nerves."

"Nerves," Gully echoed, but he sat back and was quiet the rest of the way to the school.

All of the TBYOT kids were there to help carry the gear into the gym and onto the stage. Within seconds, under Bobby Marstall's surprisingly competent direction, they were dragging speakers around and setting up microphone stands and running cords to the middle of the floor where the school's AV guy calmly plugged them into a much bigger board than Sammy's.

"Well, look at Bobby!" Sammy said to the band.

"Sometimes we all have to grow up," Julia said, running her hand nervously through her hair.

"We grow up," Gully said.

"You were born grown up," Skink told him, which made Sammy startle.

*What does Skink know about Gully? What do any of them know? Indeed—what does Gully know?* Sammy had been so busy trying to hide things, he hadn't noticed if anyone had figured it out.

"Guys . . ." he said, trying a diversion—a good enough word he supposed for what he was doing—"it's time to seriously get our act together. Consolidate." He liked the word, said it again. "Consolidate."

"It feels more like coagulate," said Julia. "None of the blood seems to be running into my hands."

"What are you two, like, talking about?" Skink looked genuinely concerned.

"Just trying to relax," Sammy said.

"Just trying to relax," Gully repeated.

"Well, you're, like, creeping me out," Skink told them. "Let's just get things done."

But there wasn't actually much for them to do as the TBYOT kids had everything sorted within minutes. Still Sammy felt the need to help, if only to keep himself from thinking about the gig.

So after dropping his clarinet case off by the stage— where it was put under the guard of a stern-faced seventh grader—Sammy went back to the car for more gear,

trailed by Gully. Skink and Julia were left checking out
the stage.

Outside, Sammy froze as Erik Addison appeared next
to the car. Looking around nervously for the other
Boyz, Sammy felt a moment of relief when he didn't
see them.

*Doesn't mean they're not around.*

Erik nodded to Sammy, said, "Hey," and then asked
Gully, "Want some help setting your drums up?" When
Gully didn't object, he grabbed the big bass drum case
effortlessly and hauled it inside.

"That's it—I'm done," Sammy said to Gully, before
turning to go back inside.

"Done," Gully echoed, carting two of the smaller
drums after Erik.

Retreating to the safety of the gym, Sammy sat down
on Skink's amp and ran scales on his clarinet, trying to
calm the elephants and butterflies.

"Ready to play?" Julia asked. She'd walked up to him
unnoticed, and now stood with her head cocked to one
side as if her fiddle was tucked under her chin. It wasn't.
She held it one-handed by her side.

He smiled crookedly up at her. "I'm not sure. It's either play or throw up."

She pretended to think about it. "I think playing would be more fun."

"If you think so." He sighed. "But tell that to my stomach."

Crouching so their faces were level, she said, "I'll tell it to you: You're going to be great. *We're* going to be great." Then, so quick that he almost didn't believe it had happened, she leaned forward and kissed him on the cheek.

Sammy's stomach turned completely over, and the elephants inside it bounced off the lining. He didn't care a bit.

Julia stood, winked at him, and turned to walk away. "Three minutes to sound check, Mr. GreenBug," she said. "And an hour till the show."

Never in Sammy's life had most of an hour passed so slowly and torturously. And never had the last few minutes gone so quickly. It felt like one second the stage manager—a senior named Tammy who seemed bored with the entire proceedings—was saying it was five

minutes to showtime, and the next second the curtain
was rising to reveal a packed house of students, parents,
and teachers, all barely recognizable behind the blaze of
bright lights.

Principal Kraft welcomed everyone and told them
how proud he was of the new eighth-grade band about to
play. He mentioned them each by name but left out the
band's name, which was something Sammy had asked
him to do.

There was a huge round of applause, some whistles,
and someone shouted out, "We love you, BUG!" And
then there was quiet, A long, ominous, scary quiet.

Sammy looked down quickly, made sure he was still
wearing his shoes.

Check.

Had his clarinet in hand.

Check.

Fly zipped.

Check.

And then he looked up, through the lights, certain
he would finally throw up, but there was no more time.
Gully was giving the four-count of the first song on his
drumsticks.

Suddenly the long hours they'd spent in the basement rehearsing kicked in and Sammy's clarinet was at his lips, his band was at his back, and the music was everywhere around him.

All he had to do was blow . . .

Sammy still had butterflies in his stomach, but he couldn't believe how well the gig was going.

The first two songs were "To Life" and "Chaim," and they went without a hitch. The band may have played them a little faster than usual, but the new tempo worked with the energy of the crowd. Each time the band took a collective breath, the audience clapped along and shouted "To Life!" and Sammy finally looked up, trying to make out the faces of his family and friends in the crowd, but the light made everyone a blur.

The quick pace of the first two songs left them with a little more time to fill, but that didn't matter because Julia went for an extra long taksim at the beginning of "Shiva" that broke the heart of everyone in the room, and got the gig back on schedule. Sammy walked out of the lights as she began to sing, and backed her soulfully on the clarinet. Skink improvised a lick in between vocal phrases that he'd never played in practice, but fit in so perfectly that Sammy couldn't believe he'd never played it before. And Gully, for once gentle on his drum kit, accented the end of a verse with a tinkling cymbal roll that sent a shiver up Sammy's spine.

With the lights all on Julia, Sammy could see into the audience now, and he happily scanned over till he found his mom and dad beaming up at him. Near them were Skink's folks dancing slow, and Julia's mother weeping openly. The rest of the crowd was rapt, weaving slowly to the hypnotic rhythm of the music, all except one large figure in the back of the room who stood stock-still, staring angrily up toward the stage.

James Lee.

Sammy was so startled, he made a squawk on the clarinet, which he had to turn into a glissando. But James Lee noticed and laughed at him.

Sammy did the only thing he could do. He closed his eyes and blanked James Lee out. Made James Lee invisible. He wasn't going to let a bully spoil Julia's solo.

*This is between the two of us*, Sammy thought. *And even if he kills me afterward, I won't have spoiled Julia's night.*

It seemed to have worked, because Sammy got back smoothly into the wailing rhythm of the song, and when they'd finished—with Julia's fiddle sounding as if it was gliding up and up and up into Heaven itself—the entire hall was quiet.

For a moment. Just a moment.

And then there was thunderous applause that broke over the stage like a tsunami.

Sammy let his clarinet drift down by his side, then walked over to where Julia was standing, grabbed the microphone, and said, "Julia Nathanson, ladies and gentlemen. She wrote that song in honor of her late grandfather."

And suddenly there was more applause. More waves of it. Maybe even bigger than the first time.

When Sammy moved back into the shadows, to let Julia take a well-deserved bow, he saw that the place where James Lee had been standing before was empty.

*Wow—I did* make him disappear.

But he'd little time to celebrate, because Gully's drumbeats ushered them right into the next song.

And then the next.

By the time they'd finished—four minutes over their allotted time because they hadn't factored in the applause—Sammy was soaking wet. Sweat had poured out of him and he hadn't noticed. He hoped no one else had, especially Julia.

When they ended with their rehearsed final introduction and shouted "BUG!" all together, the lights went out—right on cue. As they scrambled into the wings, the applause and the calls of "BUG! BUG! BUG!" from the audience were deafening.

The lights came back on, and the members of Armageddon, who'd been standing behind the scenes, sent them scurrying back for a bow.

"I wish I'd been that good at your age," the Viking-tall, long-haired blond rock god, Jon Showgrim, said to them.

Sammy was so stunned at the compliment that he stumbled, still sweating, back on to the stage, trailing the rest of the band, his clarinet clasped in his right hand.

Julia grabbed his left and then they all bowed together, hand in hand in hand in hand.

No sooner had they exited, then Bobby Marstall began issuing orders to the dark-clothed crew of seventh graders who dismantled everything that BUG owned and carted it off into the wings.

As Armageddon's crew set up their own stuff, Sammy turned to Julia and Skink and Gully. "I'm going to the bathroom. Tell my folks. I'll be right back. Then we'll really celebrate."

"We were, like, great up there," Skink said.

"I messed up on 'Chaim' though," Julia said. "Got started late and just couldn't rock it out."

"I didn't notice," Sammy said gallantly, though he had.

"Well, I did." Julia shook her head, and her dark hair covered her face for a moment, like a curtain.

"I didn't notice, either," Skink told her.

But Gully didn't—or couldn't—echo that sentiment. "You got started late," he said.

Julia turned to him, almost grateful. "Thanks for telling me the truth, Gully," she said. "I can take it." She put a hand on his arm.

"I can take it, too," Gully told her, his gray face under the gym lights had a ghostly look.

And then they were all surrounded by well-wishers, parents and students shouting their praises. Even Mr. Kraft joined in, telling them how he'd known they would be great all along.

But Sammy slipped away, heading toward the bathroom, eager to wash off some of the sweat because he wanted to be able to dance with Julia later on. *If* she would let him. *If* she'd forgive his comfortable and comforting lie.

Because it *had* been a lie. Of course he noticed she'd come in late. But she'd caught up. And they'd all flubbed something that night. Except for Gully who'd been steady as a rock on every song and totally predictable. And still—as the Big Cheese said—they'd been great.

*Great!*

Sammy was humming the "Power!" tune as he turned into the hallway that led to the bathroom, the scene of so much humiliation and yet now the place to wash off the sweat from his greatest triumph.

"It feels good to be here, now, on the winning side," he said aloud, pushing the bathroom door open.

Sammy felt blurry. No, that's not right, he thought, somewhat stupidly. My vision is blurry. And wet, too. Which didn't make much sense. How can someone have wet vision?

Suddenly Sammy realized he'd been hit in the head. That explained the blurriness.

*But why am I wet?*

Not just wet either, but totally submerged in a strange, white well of water.

*Oh wait, it's just my head that's under.* And with that he pulled himself free of the toilet bowl, realizing that he was in the school bathroom surrounded by James Lee and the Boyz.

Again.

He had just enough time to say, "Didn't enjoy the show, guys?" before his face was pushed back into the bowl. This time when he tried to pull his head back out it wouldn't budge. James Lee held him under easily.

Sammy quickly regretted wasting what little breath he'd had on a pithy comment instead of taking a big gulp of air. *Mr. Kraft was right.* He could feel he was running out of oxygen, and James Lee was showing no signs of letting him up anytime soon.

He tried to just let a few bubbles out. Just a few. But just before he thought his eyes would pop out of his head from the effort, the pressure came off and he threw himself to the side, falling to the ground, gasping and gulping and coughing up toilet water.

Around him, the bathroom was chaos. A big body was moving through the Boyz, tossing them aside, and evidently James Lee had let Sammy go to turn and face this surprising threat.

"Gully," Sammy whispered, thankful for the rescue.

Only it wasn't much of a rescue. Two Boyz grabbed their assailant from behind, and James Lee came to his feet to deliver a jackhammer blow to his stomach. Then he tossed Sammy's would-be rescuer to the floor to gasp and heave alongside him.

"Not . . . cool," Erik Addison said, clutching his stomach and looking up at his former friends. He smiled bleakly at Sammy. "Not cool to beat up such a good musician."

Sammy was too stunned to speak. And he wasn't given much time to, either, because James Lee was right back on top of him, dragging him to his knees by the hair.

"You ain't coming back up this time, Bug," he snarled.

Sammy knew James Lee was speaking the awful truth. He tried to pray, but all he could come up with was "*Shalom aleichem.*" That made him start to giggle uncontrollably, hysteria and fear being a powerful mix.

"You're bugging me, Bug," James Lee said. But before he could shove Sammy's head back underwater, James Lee was suddenly flying backward, and Gully was there in his place.

"Gully!" Sammy shouted thankfully. Then he looked at the Boyz gathering behind the golem, and at James Lee pulling himself to his feet, his eyes fearful for the first time as he calculated what massive strength it had taken to fling him halfway across the bathroom.

Suddenly, Sammy felt an anger so pure and righteous that he thought the heat of it alone could dry his hair.

"Get them," he shouted, his gesturing right hand making a circle that included everyone in the room. He was surprised that his voice could sound so cold when his every sense was aflame with rage. "Get them," he shouted again.

And Gully did.

Gully didn't move very fast, but neither was he slow, and no matter how or where the Boyz hit him, the blows seem to have no effect. They punched and grappled and kicked and tried everything they could to stop him, but Gully struck out with gray fists the size of coffee cans, and *his* blows were devastating.

Carl Fisher went down with a nose not merely broken, but shattered. Jimmy Little—who wasn't little at all—followed him to the floor with what Sammy figured had to be at least three broken ribs. Steve Schmidt stumbled out of the room leaving a trail of teeth, and his twin brother followed, hopping along on the one foot that wasn't dangling at an odd angle. Jimmy wheezed and crawled after them. The only person who got out relatively unscathed was James Lee because he'd gone for the door as soon as the first of the Boyz went down.

"Yeah!" Sammy shouted. "Nice job, Gully!"

But it looked like Gully didn't think the job was over yet. He stood over the semiconscious Carl Fisher, and casually kicked him in the stomach until the boy doubled up, putting his head in easy reach for a downward stomp that would most likely have killed him.

That kick never landed, though, because Erik staggered up from next to Sammy and launched himself into Gully. Gully rocked back ever so slightly before bouncing Erik off a urinal, his head making a dull thud that made Sammy's knees go weak.

The anger Sammy had felt mere seconds before, an anger that had seemed pure and beautiful, now felt like nothing but black bullying rage. He closed his mouth, trying not to vomit. And then he thought about chaos and fear and vengeance and blood and what they did to a person. What they did to him. He thought about Reb Chaim's warning.

"Gully, stop!" he shouted, exhausted by just those two words.

Gully turned to him, his foot once again raised over Carl's head, Erik crumpled in a heap just behind him.

"Why?" Gully asked, brow slightly furrowed, lowering his foot.

Carl recovered just enough to spot the big foot poised over his head, gasped at it, then managed to crawl out the door.

Gully watched him go impassively, then turned back to Sammy, "Why," he asked again.

"You're *killing* them," Sammy said.

Gully nodded, eyes gray and vacant. "I'm killing them," he said, and took a step toward the still unconscious Erik. "Then the bad one on the left."

*Why haven't I ever noticed how vacant his eyes are? Why haven't I noticed how scary he is?*

But it was too late for such questions. Sammy knew if he didn't have the right words now, it would be too late for anything.

He took a deep breath and reached a hand toward Gully. "No, Gully. You've done enough. I'm safe now." *Which might not be true*, he thought, *but if I don't convince Gully of that*, nobody *will be safe.*

"Not safe. Not enough. Not now." Still the blank gray eyes.

"I *command* you to stop," Sammy said.

Gully shook his head. "I am protecting you." Then his brow furrowed, as something finally showed in his eyes: confusion. "Are you the bad one on the left, too?"

Sammy's hand began to shake, and he remembered Reb Chaim's words: "A golem knows no right or wrong, only enemy and friend. You decide which is which for it now. But for how long?"

*If Gully thinks I'm an enemy to myself, will he hurt me, too?*

Sammy couldn't believe Gully would hurt him. They'd been through too much together. How could the golem turn on him now?

But then he had a flashback of Gully in the car, fist raised to punch his dad. Remembered him stalking toward Reb Chaim's office, fists clenched. Remembered him dropping the shadow that had been the dead coyote. And now he was ready to stomp the life out of Erik, who may have deserved *some* punishment—but certainly not that!

Sammy realized that if Gully stopped listening to him, no one was safe.

*Not even me.*

But what could he do? *It's not like I can overpower him and take the name of God from under his tongue.* Sammy began to shiver. *I wish Reb Chaim was here. He knows golems. He'd know what to do.*

But then Sammy had another thought: *Reb Chaim may know golems, but he doesn't know* this *golem. He doesn't know Gully.* Gully might be an uncontrollable, elemental force, but he was also a member of Sammy's band. And a friend.

*And you don't overpower your friends.* Sammy squared his shoulders. *You* talk *to them.*

Taking a deep breath, he said, "Gully, listen to me. You're my friend. You've saved me, protected me, played drums with me . . . given me a chance at a life here I didn't think was possible. And I know you want to keep on doing that."

Gully nodded and suddenly Sammy could feel tears in his eyes, blurring them even more than the water in the toilet had done. "But now *you* have become the bad one on the left. You're the one endangering me the most right now. You, Gully. You."

"Gully is the bad one on the left?"

There was suddenly something watery in those gray eyes, a mirror of Sammy's.

"Gully," Sammy said, his voice now as soft as a lullaby, "give me the paper under your tongue. The one with God's name on it."

"I cannot . . . give . . . you . . . the . . . paper. I . . ." Gully stuttered. Almost as if he were afraid, as if he knew.

"You've already protected me enough," Sammy

whispered. "Now I have to learn to protect myself. It's time, Gully. You're my best friend and I am yours. Give me the paper."

For a moment, Gully hesitated, like a toy whose batteries were wearing down. A dangerous toy.

Sammy waited one beat, two. Longer than any interval in any of the songs the band ever played. He could feel his heart thudding in his chest, and the silence stretched between them, a gulf, a canyon. He didn't dare say anything more, yet he didn't know what else to do.

But Gully did. Slowly he opened his mouth, that great gray mouth with the gray teeth and the huge gray tongue. He stuck the tongue out but made no move to take the paper out from under it.

Sammy knew then that everything was up to him. Knew it had *always* been up to him. Reb Chaim had been right all along. Standing on tiptoes, he reached into the Gully's mouth, trying not to let his fingers show how nervous he was. Those big gray teeth were much too close.

*Gully* was much too close.

At last Sammy's fingers were under Gully's tongue and he pulled the small piece of paper out. It was as dry and clean as when it had gone in. Only then did Sammy's hands begin to shake.

"You're my friend," he said again.

"You're *my* friend," Gully said. Then he began to crumble: first his feet, then his legs, a fine gray mist moving up and up until it covered his stomach and chest. A small crack widened on Gully's neck, then under his chin, and then his face began to break into small clay pieces.

"*Shalom aleichem*, Sammy," he whispered in a voice that broke on the final syllable.

And then he was gone.

All that was left was a three-inch layer of clay dust covering the bathroom floor.

"*Aleichem shalom*," whispered Sammy, kneeling down and picking up a handful of the dust. He took a fierce breath to keep from sobbing, before turning to check on Erik.

Erik was just coming to as Sammy knelt by him. He was rubbing the back of his head. "Ow."

Sammy could see a giant bump forming there.

"Give me a hand up, will ya?"

Sammy reached out, then, realizing how big Erik was, gave him *both* hands.

"That cousin of yours can sure fight," Erik said. He'd finally managed to get to his feet with Sammy's help. "Might want to let him know I'm on your side."

"Are you?" Sammy bit his lip. "On *my* side?"

Erik didn't stop to think before answering. "Yes. Yes, I am."

Trying to take a step, Erik wobbled. Sammy steadied him, throwing an arm around him for support. Though if Erik had actually collapsed, Sammy wasn't sure he could hold him up.

"What about when James Lee comes back?" Sammy asked. "Are you still on my side then?"

Erik didn't get a chance to answer. In words. But Sammy got his answer anyway, because just then James Lee came charging back into the bathroom. His face was somehow transformed. He didn't have his normal bully's sneer on. Instead, he looked angry and shamed and fearful. And moving fast.

*Like he doesn't want to come back here and face Gully, but would rather do that than go home and face his father,* Sammy thought.

True to his word, Erik shrugged off Sammy's assistance, pushing him back.

"James Lee . . ." he began, trying to step between Sammy and James Lee, but—still woozy from the blow to the head—he swayed hard left and James Lee shouldered him aside.

Sammy felt like things were moving in slow motion. He saw Erik fall again, saw James Lee closing in, his big fists clenched, his eyes scrunched up tight.

*And I'm all alone this time. Gully's gone. Erik's down. Skink's off celebrating.*

Sammy raised alarmingly small fists and stood his ground. He didn't feel brave, but there was nowhere else to go.

James Lee stepped forward and threw a hard overhand right at Sammy's nose.

In return, Sammy threw a punch of his own, an untrained uppercut that had no hope of landing, and even less hope of doing any damage if it did. He closed his eyes as he swung but instead of the expected pain of a broken nose, he felt a sharp sting in the knuckles of his right hand. He opened his eyes just in time to see James Lee falling to the ground!

Things moved very fast then. James Lee may have been down, but he was far from out. And Sammy was so stunned to have thrown a punch that landed, he just stood there staring at his momentarily downed assailant.

James Lee began to scramble to his feet, the sound coming from his mouth was more like a beast's than a human's.

Sammy guessed—*no he knew*—his end was in sight. He wondered how his parents' would take it. Tears prickled his eyes.

Suddenly there was another person in the bathroom,

moving with such speed that Sammy hardly recognized him.

Suddenly, James Lee was back on the ground, but this time he was entangled in a strange hold that involved legs and feet and his arm bent back at a near-impossible angle.

Suddenly, Sammy heard a familiar voice.

"*Shalom aleichem,*" Reb Chaim said to Sammy. Then to James Lee, "Don't move, son, or I'll have to break your arm."

"*Aleichem shalom,*" Sammy said automatically, though even to him it seemed an odd thing to say under the circumstances.

"The police are on their way," Reb Chaim said to him, but it was James Lee who answered.

"For what?" His voice was pinched and tense from obvious pain.

*But he doesn't sound defeated,* Sammy thought.

Reb Chaim chuckled. "To arrest you, I imagine. Kids started showing up in the gym hurt bad, and someone called the cops." He looked up at Sammy. "I was wrong to leave you alone to deal with this, Samson." Nodding his head toward the pile of gray dust on the bathroom floor, he said, "But it looks like you did just fine on your own."

"Hardest thing, Rabbi, hardest thing I ever did in my life," Sammy said, "but then you'd know about that."

The rabbi looked down and nodded.

At that Sammy glanced down, too, at the pile of dust in front of him He felt a huge pang of sadness. *Gully!* And then he saw what the rabbi had seen—a long, strange skid mark in the clay dust.

Suddenly smiling, Sammy realized just why it was he'd been able to connect when he threw that punch. James Lee must have slipped and skidded in the dust, his nose landing right on Sammy's fist.

*But wasn't the dust behind me when James Lee came in?* He laughed out loud. *Of course it was!*

Reb Chaim and Erik both looked at him strangely.

"You were right about golems, Rabbi," Sammy said. "But you were wrong about Gully. He protected me right to the very end. Even when it was himself he had to protect me from."

"I don't know what you're talking about, Sammy," Erik said, finally standing up by himself. "Gully's nowhere in sight. How could he have helped you?"

"Maybe I'll tell you later."

"Not going to be any later, dude. I'm taking off before the cops show up." Erik's hands were trembling, but whether from fear or just the aftermath of the blow to his head, Sammy couldn't be sure.

"And why would you want to do that, young man?" Reb Chaim asked.

*This bathroom is getting downright crowded,* Sammy thought. *And very strange. It's getting harder and harder to tell the good guys from the bad guys, whether they're standing on the left or on the right.*

Then suddenly the cop Sammy had met in Skink's hospital room was there with two other officers. Their hands were near their guns, and they looked around the room with suspicion.

"Sir," said one of the other cops to Reb Chaim, "let go of that young man right now and place your hands on top of your head."

"Wait," Sammy said as the rabbi did as instructed, and James Lee sprang to his feet. "Don't arrest him! Arrest *him!*" He pointed at James Lee.

"For what?" James Lee grinned at Sammy. "I didn't do anything."

"For . . . for . . ." Sammy stuttered.

"For assault," Erik said.

The cop from the hospital said, "He assault you? Because this kid," he gestured toward Sammy, "looks fine." His mouth curled into something like a grin. "If slightly wet."

Sammy realized how crazy it would sound if he tried to explain what had happened there. Even if he substituted a nonexistent cousin for a golem, they wouldn't believe him. He might even end up arrested for all the kids Gully had beaten up!

"Not me," Erik said, "and him." He glanced at Sammy and shot him a small smile. "But me and James Lee Joliette and a few other guys beat up a boy called Skink pretty bad the other day. I think you guys heard about that. We were wearing Power Rangers masks."

"You willing to testify to that?" the cop asked.

Erik nodded.

Sammy gulped. "You sure, Erik?"

Erik looked grim and vaguely heroic. "I told you I was on your side."

The cop from the hospital nodded to the officers who'd been about to put a pair of handcuffs on Reb Chaim. "These two," he said, inclining his head toward Erik and James Lee. "Get them down to the station." He turned to Sammy. "I'd appreciate you and your friend coming with your parents so we can talk about what happened that day." He looked around the bathroom, taking in the blood and dust on the floor. "And what happened here tonight, as well."

"Yes, officer," Sammy said, though he wasn't sure what he would tell him. *Maybe Reb Chaim will have some advice. Isn't that what rabbis are for, anyway?*

The cops took James Lee and Erik away with Reb Chaim close behind. Sammy stumbled out after them, his mind awhirl with conflicting emotions.

Suddenly Skink appeared, asking what had happened. Julia, too, putting a hand out toward him, but not actual touching his arm.

"Are you okay, Sammy?" she asked. "I swear if you're hurt, I'm going to eviscerate James Lee."

"Good word," Sammy said. "Bad idea."

And then they were all laughing, and Sammy was telling them how Erik tried to save him, and that Gully was the one who did the deed.

"But he's . . ." Sammy's voice cracked slightly, "gone now."

"Gone?" Julia asked.

*Gone. Such a short, nothing word. Four letters, one syllable. And yet it hurts so much.*

Sammy nodded and searched for a lie to tell them, something that would explain why Gully had been here one moment and gone the next. But not only couldn't he think of a believable tale, he also realized he didn't want to lie to his friends anymore.

*Yet if I tell them the truth, can they handle it?* He shook his head. They might think he was crazy, and he might lose them because of that. *But . . . I need to be truthful or I'm not being a* real *friend.*

He drew himself up. *Crazy time!* he told himself, trusting them to understand.

"Gone back to the Czech Republic?" Julia asked.

"Farther than that," he told them. "But let me tell you where he came from before I tell you where he's gone . . ."

And slowly, painstakingly, openly he did.

That they believed what he said—and later Erik did, too—amazed him. But they'd all seen Gully in action on the drums, in the classroom, and Erik had remembered a bit of what Gully had done in the bathroom. A little, but not the last bit, not when he'd been turned into clay dust. Telling that was the hardest part of all, especially with the clay still coating his shoes, his jeans. But with a catch in his throat, Sammy made it through the telling.

They were all silent for a moment before Julia said, "There was always something *otherworldly* about him. I never really thought he was from the Czech Republic actually." Then she smiled.

*It was*, Sammy thought, *a friend's forgiving smile.*

"Otherworldly," Skink agreed. "Or maybe *Under*worldly."

It was their last word on the subject then, but not the final word. Sammy had that, months later, at his bar mitzvah.

*Sammy's Bar Mitzvah Speech*
*and What Happened After*

"Shabbat shalom, everybody. It is a wonder that I am here today at all, as my parents and Reb Chaim can attest. *Attest*—that's a great word. I collect great words. Attest means to affirm or assert or authenticate. And my parents and Reb Chaim can do all that about how I got to this place and this space.

"I have a story to tell you. It has to do with my namesake, Samson of the Bible, and the story of Samson which is my Torah portion as well.

"When Samson was born, his mother was so happy, she promised an angel she would raise him as a Nazirite. Now that's a word I had to look up. Nazirites were consecrated to God. As a sign of this consecration, they never ever cut their hair. In exchange, they sometimes got extraordinary powers. The angel promised Samson's mother that Samson would become very strong—the strongest man in the world—and help deliver the Israelites from the hands of the Philistines who ruled them.

"Well, as Samson grew up, he turned into a truly big, powerful guy. Nobody messed with him. The Torah says he single-handedly killed over a thousand Philistines in a battle using just the jawbone of a dead donkey. Wow! That was a big deal. For the man *and* for the donkey. And I guess, for all those dead Philistines and their families, too.

"For twenty years, Samson led the Israelites. He was considered by them to be a good man, a fair man, as well as a strong man. The Philistines sure didn't think of him that way. That's what happens with power.

"In some ways Samson was the Israelites' golem. I doubt you all know about golems. The golem was a man made of clay and then animated by the name of God, and his only task was to save the Jews of old Prague who were being beaten and imprisoned and murdered just for being Jewish. Maybe the story of the golem was simply a folktale about power, power wielded at the start for the good. A folktale. Or a parable. Or a fantasy story. Or all three."

Sammy paused for a deep breath, looked over at the rabbi who nodded and mouthed, "Good point."

"The problem is *that* kind of power corrupts. The abused person wants one good day, one day without abuse. Reb Chaim told me this. He said about the Prague golem, that 'one good day turns into a thousand bad ones.' He meant that relying on someone else to fight your battles means that you are beholden to evil.

"So was Samson right to lead the Jews against an oppressor? Absolutely. Was he right to kill a thousand men? That's where things get fuzzy. Is killing an enemy *always* good? And what is an enemy, really, but a friend you haven't yet made. What if instead of *killing* those thousand men, Samson had laid down the jawbone and invited them to a conversation? Trading jawbones, you might say? I don't know. We only have that Biblical tale. The other side of it . . ." Sammy shrugged. "Well, that's all rabbinical commentary.

"And the reason I tell you this story? I was in a situation where I was oppressed. You all know *that* word. It means downtrodden, abused, helpless, mistreated. I was bullied in school. Bullied because I was smart and mouthy and small. An easy target. Bullies love to pick on anyone different and I was certainly different. I was the Other.

"After the third or fifth time my head had been pushed into the toilet—

"I hear you gasping, but I mean that literally for I got to know the toilet in the boys' room at my high school intimately. By the third or fifth time I knew what I wanted. I wanted a golem to be my protector. A Samson. A big guy carrying the jawbone of a donkey.

"What I found instead were friends. And we founded a band, a klezmer/jazz/pop/rock fusion band. In making music, we found our own kind of power. Creativity *is* power. Friendship *is* power.

"So, I'd like to call up those friends now, and we will play two songs for you here. The first is about power. When I asked if we could do so, Reb Chaim reminded me that King David himself sang and danced before the ark of God, so it's not a disrespectful thing to do up here on the bimah. Though we'll do it unplugged. After all, I promised my mom.

"The song 'Power!' has two new verses, which I've written just for this speech, and even the band hasn't heard them yet. The new words go like this:

*But power when it's not in check*
*Can leave your life an awful wreck,*
*Turns success right into drek.*
*Power!*

*With love and friendship, side by side,*
*We can find a better guide,*
*Not just with power, but with pride.*
*Power!*

"The second song is about mitzvah—which means a good deed. And *tzedakah*, which is about charity and mercy and doing something for all the underprivileged in the world, which is really what a bar mitzvah should be about. And when we're done, you're all invited to my bar mitzvah lunch in the rooms below. After eating, we'll play some more for you. Plugged this time. Sorry, Mom, but it's *my* party and *my* band!

"Oh—and as part of the good deeds we are asked to do in honor of a bar mitzvah, I have talked the band into playing once a month for free in nursing homes and for children in hospitals in the area. I have already set that up, and we have twelve free gigs in as many months ahead. You can find out all about that at your seat downstairs. My principal, Mr. Kraft, helped us get in touch with all those places. And if you want to add some money to give to the hospitals and nursing homes, there are envelopes by every place setting, and we will pick those up and distribute those as well.

"So, Julia and Skink and Erik—come on up. Skink plays guitar, Erik is on drums. Julia—she's the pretty one on fiddle. And I'm on clarinet.

"And we are BUG. You will find out why later.

"As a friend of mine—a real good friend to all of us in the band—used to say, *Shalom aleichem*."

As Julia and Skink and Erik took their places on the bimah, Sammy stepped forward to adjust his microphone. Erik raised his drumsticks and started the count.

"One, two, three . . ."

### Mitzvah

*The bigger the hole,*
*The longer to fill.*
*The deeper the valley,*
*The higher the hill.*
*The wider the longing,*
*The louder the cry.*

*Who's willing to help?*
*I am.*
   *And I.*

*The bigger the bully,*
*The weaker the boy.*
*The greater the sorrow,*
*The better the joy.*
*The harder the hardship,*
*The more we must try.*
*Who's willing to help?*
*I am.*
   *And I.*

*Chorus:*

*There's not enough time*
*To fill every hole;*
*Not enough tzedakah*
*For every soul.*
*But the greater the need,*
*The more we must try.*
*Who's willing to help?*
*I am.*

And I.

The wider the sea,
The smaller the boat.
The greater the need,
The weaker the hope.
The longer the illness,
The sooner you die.
Who's willing to help?
I am.
And I.

The littler the child,
The larger the love.
The bigger the eagle,
The smaller the dove.
The farther we go,
The nearer we get.
The greater the stakes,
The more we must bet.

Who's willing to help?
I am.
And I.

*And I!*

*AND I!*

*EVERYBODY:*

*WHO'S WILLING TO HELP SAY—*
*AND I!!*

Bobby Marstall stood up first. Then one by one so did each of the kids from the seventh and eighth grades, all of whom had come to the bar mitzvah. They shouted out, "And I!"

After that, the Big Cheese and Ms. Holsten stood and called out, "And I!"

Next Sammy's mother and father, tears running down their cheeks, stood up. And Sammy's uncle Freddy, the musician who'd come all the way from Hartford. And the major and the general, both clapping loudly, Julia Nathanson's two moms, and Erik's dad. And then everyone in the congregation.

From the far side of the bimah, Reb Chaim came over and whispered to Sammy, "And I." Then he raised his hands above his head and began to sway.

Sammy nodded and was about to play a trill

that signaled the last chorus, when he heard a deep, uninflected echo from somewhere overhead.

"And I."

*Gully?* Sammy waited, but there was nothing more.

He turned and looked at the band. Julia was smiling. Skink nodded and mouthed, *"Aleichem,* buddy." Erik hit his drumsticks together. "Thanks. God speed, Bugman."

With a smile, Sammy blew one last, long note that slid up and up and up like an angel winging toward heaven. Then he led his band into the final chorus.

# Songs from BUG

## Speaking with Chaim

*Going down the road*
*In the bar mitzvah bus,*
*Boogie and klezmer*
*And fusion 'R' Us.*
*Making some music*
*And making a fuss.*
*Going on down the road.*

*Chorus:*
*Going down the road,*
*Going down the road.*

*Rolling and rocking*
*To get there on time.*
*Learning some Hebrew*
*And rhythm and rhyme.*
*Trying some Hebrew,*
*And speaking with Chaim.*
*Going down the road*
*(Chorus)*

## To Life

To life, to life,
I'll bring the clay to life.
Frankenstein, he made a monster,
and made a monster's wife.
He robbed the local graveyard,
which caused some local strife.
Then villagers attacked him
With pitchfork, ax, and knife.
But me I won't be troubled, 'cause
I'll bring this clay to life!

Golem . . . golem . . . golem . . .

To life, to life,
I'll bring the clay to life,
And it will help me stop all wars
And arguments and strife.
They'll be an end to bullying,
They'll be an end to rife.
And me, I won't be troubled more,
'cause all I have to do is
bring this clay to life!

## Soul Power, Klez Style

*I've been up and I've been down,*
*I've been beaten all around.*
*I've been kicked upon the ground.*
*Power!*

*I've been hit and I've been named.*
*I've been dissed and shook and shamed.*
*And it's all a power game.*
*Power!*

*Chorus:*
*You don't have it,*
*So you want it.*
*Once you get it,*
*Then you flaunt it.*
*If you use it,*
*Don't abuse it.*
*You will lose it.*
*Power!*

*Take the power in your hands,*
*It's YOUR turn to make demands.*

*Rule the kingdom and its lands.*
*Power!*

*Come on brothers, side by side,*
*In an army long and wide.*
*We won't wait for time nor tide.*
*Power!*

*Chorus*
*But power when it's not in check*
*Can leave your life an awful wreck,*
*Turns success right into drek.*
*Power!*

*With love and friendship, side by side,*
*We can find a better guide,*
*Not just with power, but with pride.*
*Power!*

## Shiva

It's been a year, Papa, your candle glows.
And where you've gone to no one knows.
The candle flame blows high and higher,
I see your dear face in the fire.
You are my first death. Now you're gone.
We do not forget, but life goes on.

Life goes on, I'm not sure why,
Just watch me Papa from on high.
Life goes on, for me not you,
I'm singing now full klezmer blue.

Candlepower and candle flame,
I carry your soul if not your name.
I carry your love inside my heart
And know that we're not really apart.
You're here, Papa, though you have gone.
We never forget, though life goes on.

## Bar Mitzvah

*Today I am a man; I am a man today.*
*I think of many manly things; I have no time to play.*
*My voice is very deep; my thoughts are quite deep,*
    *too.*
*I am a man today. I have no time for you.*

*I've put down childish things; I've taken up the*
    *sword.*
*I skewer with a phrase; I pinion with a word.*
*Today I am a man; I have two feet of clay.*
*I am a grown-up now; I have no time to play.*

## God's Ears

*Wishing on a starry night,*
*I wish I could, I wish I might,*
*Wish away my deepest fears.*
*May wishes reach into God's ears.*

*When things go wrong, when nothing's right,*
*It's then I wish with all my might*
*And hope that someone somewhere hears.*
*Do wishes reach into God's ears?*

*Chorus:*
*Grandma said, and Grandma knows*
*The way that wishing always goes,*
*Sometimes the devil only hears*
*What your lips send to reach God's ears.*

*The best of wishes, they are those*
*You make to heal another's woes.*
*The ones to soothe your brother's fears*
*Go from your lips straight to God's ears.*

## BUG

*You can quit or you can play,*
*You can leave or you can stay.*
*If you name it, then you shame it,*
*BUG!.*

*You can fear it, or you can own it.*
*You can dull it, or you can hone it.*
*If you name it, then you shame it.*
*BUG!*

*You can run, or you can fight.*
*You're not wrong if in the right.*
*If you name it then you claim it.*
*BUG!*

## Mitzvah

*The bigger the hole,*
*The longer to fill.*
*The deeper the valley,*
*The higher the hill.*
*The wider the longing,*
*The louder the cry.*
*Who's willing to help?*
*I am.*
    *And I.*

*The bigger the bully,*
*The weaker the boy.*
*The greater the sorrow,*
*The better the joy.*
*The harder the hardship,*
*The more we must try.*
*Who's willing to help?*
*I am.*
    *And I.*

*Chorus:*

*There's not enough time*
*To fill every hole;*
*Not enough* tzedakah
*For every soul.*
*But the greater the need,*
*The more we must try.*
*Who's willing to help?*
*I am.*
   *And I.*


*The wider the sea,*
*The smaller the boat.*
*The greater the need,*
*The weaker the hope.*
*The longer the illness,*
*The sooner you die.*
*Who's willing to help?*
*I am.*
   *And I.*


*The littler the child,*
*The larger the love.*
*The bigger the eagle,*
*The smaller the dove.*

*The farther we go,*
*The nearer we get.*
*The greater the stakes*
*The more we must bet.*

*Who's willing to help?*
*I am.*
   *And I.*
      *And I!*
         *AND I!*
*EVERYBODY:*
*WHO'S WILLING TO HELP SAY—*
   *AND I!*

# Glossary of Yiddish/Hebrew Words

**Adonai:** The holy name for God in Hebrew.

**Alefbet:** The Hebrew alphabet.

**Alef:** The first letter in the Hebrew alphabet.

**Aleichem shalom:** "Upon you be peace." A Hebrew greeting.

**Bar Mitzvah:** Hebrew. This literally means "one who has the obligation of fulfilling commandments," so it marks the time when a boy is old enough to understand and become responsible for following certain rules of living. There are certain religious rites in the synagogue in which the boy takes part, in both Hebrew and his own language. And then, most often, there is a celebration or party afterward.

**Bat Mitzvah:** Hebrew. The girl's version of bar mitzvah.

**Bimah:** Hebrew. This is the platform in the synagogue where the Torah scroll is read aloud.

**Drek:** Yiddish for trash, junk.

**Frask:** Slap in the face.

**Grober:** A crude person.

**Hebrew:** A Semitic language, now seen as a Jewish language.

It is the "Holy tongue," the language of the Hebrew Bible, which Christians and others call the Old Testament, but Jews do not. It is one of the official languages of Israel (the others being Arabic and English). From the nineteenth century on, Hebrew was reinvented and revived by Eliezar Ben Yehuda and became the spoken language of Israel.

**Kavod:** Hebrew for honor.

**Kelev:** Hebrew for dog.

**Klezmer:** Jewish folk music.

**Livyatan:** The Hebrew word for whale.

**Minyan:** Hebrew for ten adult Jews, the number necessary for prayer services. In the old days they had to be men, but in the Reform and some Conservative synagogues, woman can now be in the minyan as well. The Orthodox Jews still exclude women from the minyans.

**Mitzvah:** Hebrew meaning a good deed.

**Mossad:** "The Institute" The Israeli intelligence agency responsible for counter-terrorism and paramilitary operations.

**Nazirite:** An ancient type of Jewish ascetic, typically they were forbidden to ever shave or cut their hair.

**Philistines:** Ancient people of the southern coast of Canaan before the arrival of the Israelites.

**Rabbi:** Hebrew word literally comes from the Hebrew word rav which means "master." By that term was meant someone who was a master of the Torah and the teachings of Judiasm, a sage, a scholar, a teacher. For the most part these days the term is used for a Jewish religious leader with or without his or her own congregation. Reb is the shortened form, used informally.

**Rabbinical:** Pertaining to a rabbi, usually used for teachings, wisdom, or rulings about Jewish law/customs.

**Shabbat shalom:** Hebrew greeting on Shabbat or the Sabbath, which in Judaism is celebrated from sundown on Friday evening to sundown on Saturday evening.

**Shablul:** The Hebrew word for slug.

**Shalom:** The Hebrew word for peace, which is also used as a greeting and a farewell.

**Shalom aleichem/Aleichem shalom:** Hebrew which means "Peace be upon you,/ To all of you, peace." It is used both as a greeting and a farewell.

**Shiva:** a week-long period of mourning after a death where the family stays at home and visitors come with food and comfort.

**Shul:** Place of worship, another word for temple or synagogue.

**Skullcap also called yarmulke or kepi:** The traditional Jewish head covering.

**Synagogue:** Place of worship, another word for temple or shul.

**Taw:** The last letter in the Hebrew alphabet.

**Temple:** Place of worship, another word for shul or synagogue.

**Torah:** A term that specifically means the Five Books of Moses: Genesis, Exodus, Leviticus, Numbers, Deuteronomy. Usually referring to the scroll written in Hebrew, but can mean the printed text as well. Christians refer to this as the Old Testament but Jews do not.

**Torah portion:** The section of the Torah corresponding to the date of the bar mitzvah boy's birth and read aloud by him, then talked about in his speech.

**Tzedakah:** The Hebrew word meaning charity.

**Yahrzeit:** Lighting a candle at the year's commemoration of a loved one's death.

**Yiddish:** the language of Eastern European Jews made up from medieval German and including words from Hebrew, Romance, and Slavic languages. At one point, actually up until the mid-twentieth century, it had a vibrant culture, a literary and poetic tradition, newspapers printed in the language, as well as stage plays and songs.